A LANCASTER AMISH STORM COLLECTION

Volumes 1-3 of the Lancaster Amish Storm Serial

RUTH PRICE

ISBN: 1530434564
ISBN-13: 978-1530434565

For He commandeth, and raiseth the stormy wind, which lifteth up the waves thereof. They mount up to the heaven, they go down again to the depths: their soul is melted because of trouble. They reel to and fro, and stagger like a drunken man and are at their wits' end. Then they cry unto the Lord in their trouble, and He bringeth them out of their distresses. He maketh the storm a calm, so that the waves thereof are still. Then are they glad because they be quiet; so He bringeth them unto their desired haven.

—Psalm 107: 25-30

TABLE OF CONTENTS

ACKNOWLEDGMENTS

All Praise first to the Almighty God who has given me this wonderful opportunity to share my words and stories with the world. Next, I have to thank my family, especially my husband Harold who supports me even when I am being extremely crabby. Further, I have to thank my wonderful friends and associates with Global Grafx Press who support me in every way as a writer. Lastly, I wouldn't be able to do any of this without you, my readers. I hold you in my heart and prayers and hope that you enjoy my books.

VOLUME ONE

CHAPTER 1

The air is damp, musty; leaves rotting into the muddy fields. Thick gray clouds gather between the Pocono Mountains to the north and the Delaware River to the east.

Trapped.

Ice freezes in sheets over the roads, in spikes clinging to the bare Longfellow pine branches. The creeping cold settles around Zach's shoulders. In the set of his deep blue eyes, I can see he also knows that something is coming.

Something bad.

Something that would change the life he's always known, the life we've always known together. It's been idyllic here in Lancaster. Seasons roll peacefully into one another, like colors gently fading: the green of spring, the bright blue of summer, the golden autumn, then winter's chilly white.

But now, gray has come to Faith's Landing. There is tumult, unrest, sorrow, churning and gathering, storing up its power, feeding on the ceaseless roll of the Earth. But it waits, not ready to strike.

No, not yet, those clouds seem to be thinking, as I look up at them. *Soon, but not yet.*

And I know Zach feels it too. We've known each other for so long, been through so many of those lovely seasons; I swear, sometimes we can hear each other's thoughts. It's just a closeness that comes with time, with shared experience, and a similar world view.

It's love. From before I'd ever heard the word love, before I had a mind strong enough to define love, I have always loved Zach. We were born and raised here in Faith's Landing. We were schoolmates, and he helped me with my studies. We always ate together after Sunday services, no matter whose house it was. On those days when my family, the Lapps, would have the services, I was always so nervous that everything goes just right. I even pretended, on occasion, that it was my house, not my parents' and that Zach and I were married, hosting Sunday services in a house of our own.

It may sound childish. I know it sounds that way, even to me. But those were just the seeds of love, planted into soil when it was young and fresh. And the seed was strong, ready to take root, just as in Jesus' parable. There were never any thorns or thickets to impede the growth of our love, no stone road or buggy wheel to crush us before we could realize our mutual dream.

Until recently.

Now the skies of our childhood are clouded with heavy gray, slowly creeping over our horizon, blotting out the sun. It's been long coming, I'm afraid. I look up at those heaving, rolling clouds, and feel that I've seen them before.

'In Zach's eyes,' I tell myself. *'On those quiet nights in the fields or on the porch swing. He's been so distant.'*

Slipping away.

I look up at those clouds, feel the wet winds hitting me from the east with a growing potency of their own, and I'm afraid. I'm afraid that when the storm finally does come, it's going to wash everything away, everything we've known, and everything we are.

Everything.

"Katie?" my mamm calls from inside. "You come on back inside, 'for you catch your death.'"

I take a deep breath and look around: the haze seeping over the eastern white pines, the grassy valley sloping inward. A chill runs through me, but it's not from the wind.

'Catch your death,' I repeat silently, not sure why it rings in the back of my mind with such resonance.

I turn and head back into the house. I have a quilt to finish and a venison stew to prepare. And I'm grateful for the quilts that bring us warmth in these chilly seasons, for the stew that keeps us nourished and strong, for the family that needs these things.

I'm also glad because they'll take me away from my worry for a time, remind me that there is still light to gather against the growing storm. I only hope to ignore the sorrowful flashes that remind me how much I have to lose.

So, I start chopping the carrots and potatoes, eyes locked on the chopping block and well away from the window, to better ignore the clouds. The slow rumbles, nearly inaudible, send my skin shivering. *'No, I must be imagining things,'* I tell myself. *'Not thunder.'*

Not yet.

I turn away from the coming storm, clouds gathering in my stomach to match those outside: ominous, threatening, and getting worse every second.

I suppose this is what Zach's been feeling, a storm raging within, inescapable. If only he could have explained it this way! But how could he? He doesn't understand it himself.

***

Two miles from where Katie is standing, Zach fights the storm that's been so long in coming.

The storm within.

4

It has been raging for months, ever since his period of *rumspringa* began last year. He had thought that a few weeks of exploring Englischer life would satisfy him.

But the storm only grew.

And it's still growing.

Pounding a new fence post into the soil on the east boundary of the Yoder farm, even Zach's brother, Isaac, can't help fight the rising tide of Zach's discontent. Isaac hopes more and more simply to prevent Zach from drowning in it, or being dashed to bits on rocks of his own unhappiness.

"Fences," Zach mutters, as they drive the post in, mallets punching the flat tip of the pine beam deeper into the ground.

"Gotta have fences," Isaac said.

"Oh yeah, Farmer John, and why's that?"

Isaac chuckles a bit, then offers up a casual shrug. "Keep things out, keep things in."

"Precisely, Isaac, that's exactly what I've been talking about. That's what's wrong with this whole community, this whole country! Everybody's so busy keeping everybody in, and everybody else out ... I hear people in the city live their whole lives without ever knowing their neighbor's names."

"All the more reason not to live in the city."

"Well, are we any better? We're so isolated from the

Englischers. After rumspringa, we're either in or out and that's it. If they can't keep you in, they kick you out."

"Well, it's not as mean-spirited as all that," Isaac says, setting the mallet down. "Putting you through the fire is the congregation's final way of telling you that they love you." After a skeptical silence, Isaac adds, "It's a lot more care and concern than you'll find from that lot of strangers and thieves out there."

"You really buy into all that hobgoblin bologna everyone keeps dishing out around here?"

"Zach — "

"Isaac, there are a lot of good people out in the world; caring, decent, loving, trustworthy people."

"Of course there are —"

"But you'd judge them, at just sixteen years old, because they choose to drive cars, or go to churches on Sundays, and not worship in private homes, as we do."

"No, Zach," Isaac says, calm to counter Zach's growing ire, "they can do as they like. And so can I; so can we. And we do."

"And so can I."

"I know," Isaac says, as they lift the crossbeam into place. "That's what worries me."

"Don't you think I can make it out there on my own? I'm your older brother, Isaac. I'm the one who should be worrying about you!"

Isaac says, "I think you can make it out there just fine, Zach. But I don't think it'll bring you happiness. Traveling is a fool's paradise, Zachariah. I think you're trying to escape something that's deep within, something you can never outrun, something you can't keep hiding from."

Zach shakes his head as they stroll back toward the house, heels sinking into the soft ground. "My brother, the poet. And yet, I'm the one who wants to run off to an Englischer school."

Isaac shrugs. "There's nothing I can learn in their world that I can't learn here. Nothing I'd want to learn, anyway. What I don't really get is, why you'd want to leave."

"But you *like* farming, Isaac."

"Sure do; love it! The feel of the dirt; the smell of the morning; the flavor of the food." He takes a deep breath and lets it spill out of his smiling nostrils. "Those city people haven't a clue what they're missing."

Zach smiles at his younger brother, enjoying the boy's maturity, his calm. Isaac was always the most sedate of the two, the most diligent. Zach was the one with all the energy, the restless spirit, the creative streak, the romantic. Zach's the one with dreams too big for what his life here has prepared him to lead. While there are programs to help bridge the gap between

7

his current level of education, having only completed the eighth grade, it's like he's standing with his nose pressed to the window of a wider, more brightly colored world that he can only see a fraction of, standing outside.

Isaac adds, "It's so simple here. It's nice. I'm gonna marry Beth, take over the farm, look out for Daed and Mamm, raise a passel of youngsters; it's gonna be great. I wish you'd stick around, do the same. We'd both make great uncles."

"Ja, that sounds great, Isaac, really." But Zach gazes out over the fields, the thick clouds getting taller, broader, and scarier. "I just don't know ... if it's right for me..."

"What'd you have in mind?" Isaac asks. "Be a rock star? Astronaut? International jewel thief?"

"See Paris," Zach says, "study history, write a book. Isaac, there's a whole big, wonderful world out there, just waiting to be explored, begging to be seen and experienced!"

"Okay, Christopher Columbia, take it easy." They share a chuckle. "Anyway, if you want to go to college, go to college."

"You know, it's not that simple," Zach says. "Mamm, and Daed especially."

"And Katie."

Zach turns. "What's Katie got to do with it?"

But Isaac just looks at Zach, with that knowing expression that says more than words can. Zach needn't have asked. Katie has everything to do with it.

CHAPTER 2

Zach comes to me the next day, while I'm hanging the laundry out to dry. Those gray clouds hover over me, promising a flood of biblical proportions, but not offering even a teasing trickle.

Not yet, I can almost hear them say.

Which is just as well, as I've got two loads of laundry that I hope will be dry by the end of the day.

Zach shares his thoughts and doubts with me, as he has before. Of course! We're best friends, soul mates, destined to be together through life. It's only natural that he'd share his thoughts with me, and that I'd support him in any way that I could.

But there's no point in me denying that I want Zach to stay, marry me, and raise a family with me, here in Faith's Landing. I don't want to live out *there*. I think Isaac is right, that Zach has to face whatever it is that is troubling him inside his soul, and not go seeking for a remedy somewhere in a stranger's arms, or some filthy inner city somewhere.

This is where he belongs, with me.

The only problem is, I can't say that to him, because I'm not unselfish in my perspective. I even challenge myself, in a voice I try to contest, but can never escape. It's the one voice I know I can't deceive: my own.

'You want him to stay for you, not for him,' I chide myself

'No,' I object. *'I believe this is where he belongs, that the world outside is better left to those who created it. That's not our world; it's not our place.'*

'But Katie, you know he has to discover that for himself.'

And this is where I always stop, because there's nothing more I can say; not to myself, not to Zach. I have to encourage him to follow his heart, his dreams, his faith; and hope and pray that they all lead him straight into my arms.

Zach says, "I know how you feel about it, about me living on the outside, leaving Lancaster."

"Well, I, um ..." I'm locked between the truth of my faith in his ability, my wish for his happiness, and my desire for his hand in marriage.

Trapped.

And this moment, as I stumble into a tiger pit with my foot

firmly implanted in my mouth, seems to stretch on forever. And the longer it goes on, the deeper the pit and the slower my fall. Finally, I clear my throat and say, "We're friends, Zach, and whatever you want, that's what I want for you. And if what you want is to learn a bunch of things —"

"Well, of course I want to learn a bunch of things, Katie. Don't you?"

I search my mind, my heart, and my soul. "I ... I think I know what I need to know ... so far, I mean. The rest, I'll learn along the way. That's the way life is, a prolonged learning experience. I mean, why go to college, when life is like college itself, college that goes on and on?"

Zach chuckles a bit. "You're talking about experience, Katie, not education."

"Learning is learning, isn't it? And the stuff you learn from experience, that's the stuff you need, the stuff you use every day: how to deal with people, how to sew and harvest and care for your family, your community. Those are the things that really matter, Zach, to me, at least."

"Those things matter to me, too."

"And what does your Englischer education offer that experience doesn't? The names of a lot of dead people; dates of wars and assassinations; old speeches that were mostly lies in the first place. Is that what you're so keen on?"

"You really think that's all there is to it?" Zach asks me,

even though I don't take it for a question. It's a contradiction. "The entirety of human thought: science and philosophy, history, poetry, literature, architecture, mathematics. These are part of our shared human heritage. To shut ourselves off from these things is to deny something vital and wonderful inside ourselves, and inside each other."

"But, in pursuing them, aren't we sacrificing something even more wonderful, our innocence and our sense of wonder?"

"I just don't think so, Katie. Open your eyes, and they see more, and they open ever wider. Shut them, and they may stay shut forever. I want to live with my eyes open. I just don't see why our community wants us to shut them at the age of fourteen, when we still know so little of the world."

I've never given it much thought, but, as I reflect on it, an answer comes to me. "Experience takes over where education leaves off."

"We can have both, Katie." He smiles, and I feel like I want to die.

"I really think you should just pray on it, Zach," I say, pinning a white apron to the line. "Now mine eyes shall be open, and mine ears attend unto the prayer that is made in this place."

"Second Chronicles 7:18 notwithstanding, I have been praying, Katie. That's part of the problem." Reading my confusion, he goes on to say, "Well, praying's not the problem, obviously. It's the answers I'm getting, or rather ... *not* getting. I feel like God isn't listening to me anymore, or He's not responding. Or if He is, I just don't understand Him the way I used to, the way I always assumed I did."

I turn, resting my palm comfortingly on his upper arm, the words of Isaiah 64:8 rising from my heart to my lips, "Zach, it's not for us to understand God, but to love Him, obey Him, be faithful. 'But now, O Lord, thou art our father; we are the clay, and thou our potter; and we all are the work of thy hand.'"

Zach looks me deeply in the eyes, those gray, sorrowful clouds obscuring the green. "If I knew what God wanted me to do, I'd obey. If I knew where God wanted me to be, I'd go."

"Or stay."

"Yes," he says, after what I think is a dangerously long pause, "or stay."

I search my mind for some way I can convince Zach to see that this is where God wants him to be, for something I can point out, or remind him of.

Something I can offer.

It's not the first time that the idea has occurred to me, of course. All this time around Zach, knowing him and loving him as I do, and with my body aging through its teenage years and on to adulthood, I'd have been crazy not to think about it a little. It's only natural to have certain impulses, certain cravings; but being Amish means we don't relinquish control of our bodies over to our bodies themselves. Our minds must govern our bodies, our strength of will, our faith in God.

And, so far, we've both been observing our shared Amish traditions. We've kissed, but nothing more than that. But I'm growing up now, and growing up means facing your fears, as well as your desires and responsibilities. It means turning to face the man I love, and showing him that I love him.

No, I hear a familiar voice echo in the back of my brain, *not yet.*

'There must be something else,' I tell myself, *'something we already enjoy.'* I want to keep our physical intimacy special and sacred, to share it with God's blessing, to live without shame in the eyes of the community, and be someone they respect and admire.

But Zach is even older than I am, and, at seventeen, his body is filled with desires that his adventurous spirit is bound to embrace. If he was restless before, all those hormones are making him even more restless now. And he's not been shy about saying so; not in a demanding way, of course. But how was it *not* going to come up?

And I've been able to distract him, so far, but the time for those distractions is running out. Every other thing leads us to that single subject: harvest festivals and hay rides, errands in the town square, even the sacrosanct Sunday services become heated with tension, as we share a meal afterward, glances shooting across the room in silent sensuality.

So, I find myself in a familiar but uncomfortable position, between our mutual desires and our differing thresholds. The stress increases on all parties until I know that something is going to give, and when it does, the whole house of cards that is our lives together may come tumbling down around us.

"If I just had a sign," Zach says. "Some way to know for sure."

"What about all the evil in the world," I ask, "the famine and the disease and the corruption? Is that really the world you want to live in?"

Zach breaks a bittersweet smile, one that is both sacrificial and life-affirming. "That world needs help, Katie. What if God's will is for me to go out there and do what I can for them? And what if, in the name of fear or laziness, I allow myself to believe that is contentedness ...?"

I can't answer him. I have no answer.

He turns and adds, "Living in doubt, I'll hate myself forever."

Again, I can't answer. Not because I don't have an answer, I just don't like it and don't want to share it, as much as I know it to be true. If I had the courage, the sense of self-sacrifice that I know true faith requires, I'd tell him to go.

But I've stopped myself from doing so, dozens of times,

since this angst crept up on Zach last year, and I reassure myself I can do it once more, if it will keep him by my side.

For a little while longer, at least.

CHAPTER 3

John and Ruth Yoder are worried about their son. The second oldest of their eight children, Zach is the first to experience this kind of rumspringa discontent. His older sister, Sarah, had barely dipped her toe in the rumspringa pond before marrying and taking the kneeling vow.

Now the peace of their household is disrupted by Zach's growing disquiet. He's stayed on the farm to help with the chores, but he goes out more and more, and is at the house less and less. His absence nurtures their doubt about his present activities, and, much more importantly, about his future.

At fifty-three-years-old, John Yoder sits among the elders in the community. It is both a privilege and a responsibility, and Zach's restlessness is starting to reflect upon John in the eyes of his peers, and of the community. He takes counsel with them on the matter from time to time, especially now that winter keeps him from working the fields, as he'd prefer to do.

There are only so many weeds to pull on a beet farm as efficiently run as the Yoder farm.

And while John is helping a fellow town elder replace the front door of his house, the elder helps him with whatever advice or wisdom he can muster on the boy's fall from grace with the Amish way of life. And since that elder is none other than Deacon Aaron Kopp, the graying, expanding, spiritual leader of the community, John could hardly go to a more qualified person to help.

The two carry the heavy cedar door into place, perpendicular to the doorway. They've already screwed the hinges into the door, and now they line up the hinges with the door jamb, wedging a beam of wood under it to hold the door in place, while they start twisting the screws into the jamb.

Deacon Kopp says, "There may be no more danger to letting him go, than in forcing him to stay."

"If he chooses to stay," John says, "then I'm not forcing him."

"*If* he chooses to stay," Deacon Kopp repeats, twisting the screw into the wood. "And if not?"

"Then he'll change his mind. He's my son, Deacon. I'm not going to let him throw his life away. I'm not letting any of my kids make that kind of mistake."

"But what mistakes will you be making in the bargain?"

John shakes his head, hoping not to show too much disrespect. "Look at us, Aaron, in our fifties now. Whatever our mistakes, what difference does it make? But Zach is just seventeen, and some mistakes, you spend your whole life paying for."

***

Back at the Yoder house, Zach sits down with his mamm, Ruth, over a plate of warm oatmeal cookies and cold milk. The living room is quiet, with Sarah moved out, baby Iris asleep in the crib, and the rest of the kids at school for the first time since the holiday.

Zach takes a bite of the cookie, moist and grainy, the raisins plump and chewy, the milk cold and delicious. But Zach can't enjoy the pleasures of the simple snack. He hasn't been able to enjoy very much lately, which inspires Ruth to sit him down at this moment of rare calm.

Ruth says, "You were out again last night. Should I ask with whom?"

"Just some Englischers I met at a concert," Zach says.

"A concert?" Ruth repeats. "Oh, my! Was it ... very loud, this concert?"

Zach can only nod. "It's rock music, Mamm; it's supposed to be loud."

Ruth tries to smile, but her downcast gaze only hides her inner sadness. This isn't a conversation she wanted to have with any of her kids, and she never thought she'd be having it with Zach. The vision of his marriage, his future life and *kinner*, it was all so fresh in Ruth's imagination, ever since Zach was so young. To think of it as mere fantasy now is heartbreaking, but not as much as the idea of seeing her son living such a sad, unfulfilled life.

Ruth says, "Are you planning any other activities for the week?" But Zach just shakes his head, taking another bite of cookie and washing it down with some milk. She adds, "Did you have a good time last night?" Zach offers only a half-smile to answer her. "Well, do you ever have a good time on these excursions? You're on rumspringa: are you enjoying it?"

Zach turns, knowing what his mother is getting at. "Mamm, Englischer life isn't all nightclubs and beer bars. It's not just about going out and having fun, any more than our lives are about constant drudgery and no electricity. It's all so much more complicated than it appears to others."

"Well, I do agree with that," Ruth says, with a considered nod. "I often wonder why people come around to gawk at us the way they do, from Jersey and New York and Philadelphia, when they think we're such sad, miserable people."

"Because they want to know the truth behind the rumors," Zach says, taking her chubby hands in his. "Because they want to see and experience things for themselves! And when they come, and they buy your beautiful quilts —"

"No, they're not —"

"Yes, they are," Zach urges her, "they are beautiful, and there's no shame in that! You are very skilled, Mamm; those skills are gifts from God. Is it wrong not to celebrate Him by celebrating them?" But this time the wordless response is hers, and he is left to dangle in the awkward silence. "And when the Englischers see how much beauty there is in our lives and in our hearts, how much freedom there is in what seems to be such a regimented way of life, isn't that a holy and blessed message for them to go away with?"

"It is. And it's well that they should go away. They don't belong here, Zach. We do."

Zach tries to smile. "*You* do, Mamm."

Ruth smiles, and touches Zach's cheek. This is the same cheek she touched when it was newborn, red and swollen. The same cheek was so soft and white, in the months and years that followed, smeared with honey and maple syrup and beef gravy, with dirt and mud and tree sap, the funny filth of childhood, the silly stuff of youthful folly.

But years drew angles into those soft, chubby cheeks, whiskers sprouting. Now Ruth has to strain to recognize the child who once stood before her. In his place, a man has appeared: a man of strength, and strength of will. A man who must find his own way, even if that means walking away from her.

Ruth tries not to cry.

Instead, she asks herself, *'How do these Englischer families do it, send their children off to have lives and families, and often see them only once or twice a year? One of the great boons of Amish life is the strength of the family bond. Families remain close, and close by. But that doesn't seem to be the Englischer way'.* Ruth must remind herself, *'They love to strike out on their own, become the self-made men their legendary forefathers were; the rugged individual'.*

'But they don't understand,' Ruth thinks. *'And how could they? They think it's all so romantic. But their forefathers were only self-made men because they had to be. And the wilds are simply too rugged for the individual; that's what makes the community so important in general, and the Amish community so important in particular.'*

'But Zach should know what they don't,' Ruth silently proclaims, herself the only audience.

Grasping at inspiration, Ruth says, "You belong here too, Zach. In my heart, I believe that's true, that it will always be true. But my heart is not the one you should follow. And what I believe to be true isn't what matters now." She rubs his cheek again, a chill running down her arm, and curling in the chambers of her heart. "What do *you* believe, Zachariah?"

Zach turns, gazing out the window, his eyes narrowing to slits as he focuses in on an imaginary distance, so clear in his imagination. "The Lord is my shepherd; I shall not want. He maketh me to lie down in green pastures: he leadeth me beside the still waters. He restoreth my soul: he leadeth me in the paths of righteousness for his name's sake. Yea, though I walk through the valley of the shadow of death, I will fear no evil: for thou art with me; thy rod and thy staff they comfort me. Thou preparest a table before me in the presence of mine enemies: thou anointest my head with oil; my cup runneth over. Surely goodness and mercy shall follow me all the days of my life: and I will dwell in the house of the Lord forever."

After a long, sad silence, Ruth clears her throat and says, "Well, um, have you given any thought to which college you'd like to attend?"

"College," John says, capturing their attention as he steps into the room. "So you can be indoctrinated into that cesspool of lies and Satanism?"

"Daed, it isn't like that at all."

"What do you know about it?" John demands. "The only reason you want to go is to find out for yourself, isn't that right? See the world. Unlike you, I have seen it, and I know what's out there. I only wish you'd allow yourself to benefit from my experience."

"That's your experience, Daed. Nobody can say that mine will be —"

"The world hasn't changed since I was in rumspringa, Zach. People don't change."

"At last, we stumble upon your true area of expertise."

Ruth says, "Zachariah!" to shush him, but she can already feel herself being squeezed out of the conversation by the opposing forces of the two men in the room. There's little she can do now, but try to keep them from coming to blows over this long-simmering conflict. Ruth decides to hold her ground, stay put, and say as little as necessary.

"Speak your peace, boy!"

"Change, Daed, you said it yourself. And around here, nothing changes ... ever! One generation into the next, same clothes, same foods, same chores, same faces, same Sunday services. But that's not life, Daed, not life the way it should be."

"You don't know what you're talking about!"

Zach's words come faster, louder, voice cracking in his desperate throat. "Life is all about change, Daed, from boys to men, girls to women, new people and new experiences, different points of view. Without change, there's only stagnation and rot. It's not really living. It's just ... existing!"

"It's living with God!" John responds. "God is not something to be cast aside, like an old shoe! Our people only deepened our faith by remaining apart, living a life based on scripture, and in harmony with nature. We are able to live happily and simply, without fear of our neighbors, because our communities are strong. Our lives are not stagnant, they are rich in the attention and righteousness of the Lord. Out there, Englischers have no common past, no ties beyond their families, and even those are strained. Is that what you want to learn? I'm only trying to stop you from making the biggest mistake of your life." Silence hangs in the stillness of the living room, before John adds, "Zachariah, what you don't understand, is what you're sacrificing now by turning your back on your past, your family, your way of life. Son, I'm only afraid that, in the years to come, from somewhere out in that world, you'll look back on the life you had here, the things you took for granted, and wish that you'd stayed."

The two Yoder men stare each other down, Ruth frozen in the tension that surrounds them. These two love each other. That's clear to Ruth, and to them as well. And love isn't the only thing they share. They share family, blood, and history.

But a future together doesn't seem to be one of those things.

Not wanting to increase the pitch of their conflict, Zach clears his throat and stands up from the table. "Thank you for the cookies, Mamm. I better get out and check those coon traps."

Zach steps past John, ignoring his father's parting dig. "Don't dawdle, don't want to be late for tonight's festivities ... whatever they are."

"Daed, I —"

"And you!" John doesn't turn to face her, but his expression is so wrought with anger that he needn't show it to her for Ruth to understand his disposition. "You're encouraging him."

"I am not," Ruth says, trying not to sound defiant, while also not wanting to fuel John's anger. "But if Zach is unhappy, and he has been for so long, shouldn't we —?"

"No, we shouldn't."

"He's my son, John. I can't stand to see him be this miserable for the rest of his life. If he decides this is what's best, if that's God's will, shouldn't we just trust in that, have faith that everything'll work out for the best?"

John looks at her, long and hard. "Shall we go without planting seeds and hope that, come harvest, everything will work out for the best? Shall we give infant Iris a gun to play with, and rest assured in faith that God's will alone will protect her?" Ruth offers no response, just as John has predicted. He goes on to say, "We're his parents, and we owe it to him to take an active part in his life, while we still can."

"Can we still?"

John looks back to the doorway, where Zach so recently passed, and through which he may never pass again. Feeling the full gravity of that terrible possibility, John says, "We can, for a brief while longer. But the less time we have, the more desperate our measures will have to be."

"John?"

"It's too much, too much freedom, for far too long." John bites his lower lip as he considers, nodding to some faint idea growing in his imagination. "It's time to make some adjustments."

Ruth tilts her head, confusion in her plump, pale face. "But he's on rumspringa. You can't make any adjustments to that."

Then, that biting lip becomes a little, mischievous smile. "We'll see."

CHAPTER 4

The next day I have a brainstorm, and head down to the Lancaster County Public Library. I haven't been there in years, and the library reminds me of childhood school excursions, when we were always so quiet and careful of our manners. As soon as I can get back to Faith's Landing, I find Zach working with Isaac, clearing the weeds from the fields.

I step up with a little basket filled with a few things I know will brighten their day.

"You fellas ready for a break?" They look up, sweating even in the chilly breeze of the encroaching storm. I open the basket and hold it out to them.

Isaac reaches in and pulls out an apple, biting greedily into it. "Thanks, Katie. If I didn't have Beth, I'd marry you in a minute!"

Zach shoots his kid brother an annoyed look, but Isaac just

shrugs and bites into the apple again. Shaking his head, Zach pulls out an apple of his own, biting into it with a smile.

I say, "That's very sweet, Isaac. How are things with Beth? You two planning anything ... significant in the near future?"

"Not yet. Soon." Isaac looks at Zach. "I thought this one might marry first, show me how it's done."

Another glare from Zach quiets Isaac.

Rolling my eyes as innocently as I can, I say, "Um, I've actually got something extra-special for you, Zach."

Isaac looks at me, then back at his brother. "Oh, okay, I'll, um, I'll go check on the barn. I'm not sure it'll hold through the winter. Excuse me?"

We nod, as Isaac strolls away, chewing on his apple. I turn as Zach faces me with an expectant expression, shoulders shrugging nearly imperceptibly. Unable to disguise my smile any longer, I pull my little gift out of my apron pocket, and hand it to him.

He looks at it, a bit confused. "A library card?"

"I went down there myself; they've got everything! More books than you'll be able to read in a lifetime, on every subject; magazines, youth books, even the internet!"

"Katie —"

"I thought about it, and I decided you were right."

"Katie?"

"Why shouldn't you learn everything you can about anything you want?"

"Katie —"

"And you can, starting right now! I thought maybe we could go together; make a date out of it. We'll go every Saturday, check out some books; they have live readings there, every first weekend of the month —"

"Was this Isaac's idea?"

"Isaac?"

"He was saying something similar, not long ago." He turns, calling, "Isaac!"

"No, no, Zach, it wasn't Isaac's idea, silly; it was mine." I let myself lean a bit closer to him, and my gaze lowers demurely to the ground. "I just want to help you, give you what you want."

He smiles. "And it's very thoughtful, Katie. Really, I do appreciate it. Sure, we can go to the library together. That sounds great."

I feel a little boost of energy to counter my disappointment. "Okay, great!" I give him a little kiss on the cheek, unable to hide my smile. "I'll let you boys get back to work." I walk back toward my buggy, parked in front of their house, as Isaac crosses me and arrives to meet Zach in the field. I look back, to notice that Zach seems to be glaring at Isaac, who has no idea why.

***

Later that day, I'm working on my new quilt in the living room. The weather is growing bleaker, the clouds gathering beyond the big scarlet oak tree that stands just outside the window. The crackling logs in the fireplace spit out bits of burning sap, to fill the room with that warm, cozy pine smell.

My kid sisters, Esther and Martha, sit on the floor, their faceless dolls on the floor between them. Esther is older, almost five, and Martha is just two. Mamm and I can barely keep our eyes on the quilt as we turn and gaze at the youngest Lapp girls, so sweet and loving to one another. They seem so much like children to me, and I feel so much like an adult when I'm around them.

But it's a bittersweet moment, because to look upon them is to be reminded that we can no longer turn and see our beloved Jacob. To hear the girls chatter is to have to imagine what things our bright young man would be saying, if that terrible buggy accident hadn't happened.

'He would have been ten years old next month,' I say to myself. I try to shake it off. *'Life is for the living,'* I remind myself, recalling Luke 9:60. *But He said to him, "Allow the dead to bury their own dead; but as for you, go and proclaim everywhere the kingdom of God."*

Where Jacob is now, he has no troubles, no worries. Where

I am, there are troubles and worries enough, and then some.

Mamm and I normally work in a quilting bee, with Gramm and other ladies of the community. But tonight it's just us two, which makes it a nice opportunity for us to share our thoughts on quilting, on life, and on boys.

On Zach.

He didn't seem that excited about the library card, and I can't help but wonder if knowledge of history and philosophy are what he's really seeking, and not knowledge of less ... scholastic pursuits.

"Have you prayed on it?" Mamm asks me, dipping her needle into the cotton of our country bride applique, a white quilt with five square designs of pale violet flowers and little green leaves. "'And Hannah prayed, and said, "My heart rejoiceth in the Lord, mine horn is exalted in the Lord —"'"

"'My mouth is enlarged over mine enemies,'" I interrupt, without meaning any disrespect, "'because I rejoice in thy salvation.' Mamm, I've prayed on it, I've told Zach that he should pray on it; I've prayed that he'd pray! Even Elijah knew that prayer could only go so far."

"Elijah went past prayer and unto praise," she gently reminds me, with an underlying sternness that warns me not to use Biblical examples if they're not completely apropos. "Elijah praised God for the rain he knew would come, even during that terrible drought, with no end in sight to the naked eye. And he was right, rain did come. It had already been decreed by God. The seeds of rain had been planted unseen by Elijah, and he knew that. Have you praised God for helping Zach see the light, as you're certain he will, as you've prayed that he would?"

"You really think that's the case," I ask, "that God has already chosen the time and place for Zach's decision, and that whatever decision that will be, God has already decided?"

"Isaiah, 46:10," she says. "Declaring the end from the beginning, and from ancient times the things that are not yet done, saying, My counsel shall stand, and I will do all my pleasure."

I give it some thought. *Surely, God is all-seeing and all-powerful; of this I haven't a doubt. And He would never allow one of his children to go astray. He didn't allow Job, or Jonah, or King David to go far astray, without bringing them back to His embrace. He protected Lot, and Daniel, and the three Hebrew children, thrown by King Nebuchadnezzar into the fiery furnace.*

Are these fires seven times hotter than they ought to be, as it was in that terrible king's mighty kiln?

I've never doubted God's will or His power before, and I don't doubt them now, even in the shadow of Zach's doubt.

But it feels unnatural for me to do nothing, simply to let God take care everything, while I sew and pray.

I ask my Mamm, "When you and Daed began courting, did you ... encourage him in any way?"

She looks at me for a moment, then back down at the quilt. "I did not." After a heavy pause, Mamm adds, "I didn't need to. Your daed and I began courting because neither of us had any doubts about the other. He didn't need any encouragement. And if he did, I would have wondered if he was the right boy for me."

"Because you would have been interfering with God's will?"

"That's right," she says, her voice growing in sternness. She can see where I'm going, in this conversation, and my imagination. She doesn't approve of either one. Mamm adds, "A woman should not use her femininity to entice a man, Katie. It's immodest and cruel."

"Cruel? Mamm, it's just natural —"

"For the man to pursue a woman is natural," she says, not needing to add the rest: that she feels any other scenario is unnatural.

And, without feeling the need to say so, I'm not sure I agree. My parents are both such old-fashioned people. And that is part of our Amish lifestyle, a part that we treasure. It's a part that frustrates Zach, who longs to break out of the old fashions, and into the new. I find myself caught between both points of view, understanding each in moderation, yet finding it harder to commit wholeheartedly to either one.

Trapped.

And the pressure is gathering around me, those clouds hovering closer, heavier, nearer to their stormy readiness.

If I take a more active part in our courtship, I often wonder, why is that so unnatural? As long as our ultimate union is the natural state of things, why is it so wrong to help things on their natural course? Even the strict John Yoder believes that one must plant a seed, and not merely pray for harvest; one must do what they can, sometimes whatever is necessary, to protect their loved ones from harm.

While I sit with my Mamm, I realize that we don't see the world precisely the same way. This is no reflection on either of our characters. We're just different people. She's Mary Lapp, and I'm Katie Lapp. We share more than just a last name—we share history, and we share blood. But we don't share everything. Everybody sees the world in a unique way, even when there are tremendous similarities, but no two people feel exactly the same way, about exactly the same things, for exactly the same reasons, any more than any two people are exactly the same person.

Even family.

Even soul mates.

No, I silently determine, *I can't just sit and do nothing while Zach slips away from me. It's fine for Mamm and Daed that things worked out so smoothly, but every situation is a little bit different, because every two people are unique. And for the two people in question, me and Zach, the remedy may be just as unique, at least as far as my family history is concerned.*

And why shouldn't it be? Why shouldn't we come together in this way? We have strong feelings for each other that we want to share. If one of us has to take the next step, why shouldn't that be me? I ask myself. And closeness between a man and a woman isn't itself an evil or wicked thing, not between two loving people, such as Zach and me. It's a natural act, consensual, and not cruel.

Cruel? I repeat, my mind sticking on the word, and its meaning.

I say to Mamm, "Why is it cruel for a woman to give herself to a man ... in that way, I mean?"

Mamm looks up from the quilt, gray eyes peering through the strands of her brown bangs, which hang tiredly out from under her bonnet. "It's a form of manipulation, Katie, to use your body as a means to force him to stay. That makes a gift of oneself into a lie, and lying is dishonest."

"But ... cruel?"

"Ja," Mamm nods, "cruel to you both. The lust of the body obscures the purity of the heart, at least for a time, but when the fires of lust have cooled, what remains, but ashes? When shared between man and wife, the physical bond strengthens the bond of marriage, but, outside of God's law, what God meant to be the ultimate expression of love becomes a trivial distraction, leading only to resentment and pain."

"I? Mamm, I'm just —"

"I know what you're just ... " she says, turning her attention back to the quilt, as if she'd rather not look at me, as if I'm not worthy to be in her sight. "For you ... or anyone... to use her body to knowingly manipulate another, perhaps change the course of his entire life —"

"But aren't these things predestined by God to happen? Mamm, you just said —"

"Enough of this, child!" Her sudden anger sends a shocked chill down my spine. Mamm rarely loses her temper, and when she does, it never fails to resonate down to my very core. "It's not so simple to say things are predestined. We were given free will, to use or abuse as we choose, but God has given us the tools to lead us to our better fate, and our better selves. When we turn away from that, when we turn to sin, we not only wound ourselves, but we wound those we say we love. If you can't understand that, then perhaps I have failed you. All of us have failed you."

We sit in the quiet of the living room, just a bit less warm and cozy than before.

It's not that I want to be wanton, but I can't lie; since I've started to become a woman, the thought of more intimate touch dominates my thoughts, as plain and omnipresent as the sky over our heads, or the Earth beneath our feet. Everywhere I turn, every step I take, the thought is inside me, a ceaseless pounding that shakes my resolve, and leaves my body quivering, my faith rattled, and my walls that much closer to crumbling.

And they haven't been without siege. Zach has been wanting to scale these walls for some time, and only the social forces suppressing our desire had any real effect. Left to our own devices, it's hard to imagine that faith alone would have been enough to keep us chaste.

And now those social pressures, the views of our parents, and even our siblings and friends, seem to be weakening, as we're given leave to explore our interests for our rumspringa. Even the Bible is rife with fornication and lust, although it only rarely works out to the benefit of those involved. Such things are often punished in the Old Testament, and cautioned against in the New Testament, something I try to keep in mind as my body offers more and more distraction.

But it's a distraction I could ignore for a while, yet. I'm not personally enduring the kind of soul-searching strife that my beloved Zach is, or feeling the kind of pain that he's feeling. It's his trial that concerns me now; his needs, not my own. Our desires may be the same, even if our compulsion differs a bit.

But I'm increasingly willing to overlook my own patience

in favor of his urgency, my own preference for his undeniable hungers. For they cannot be denied: this seems certain. Waiting and denial are tearing Zach apart, and I'm afraid he simply won't be able to endure much more.

I can't help but wonder: where will Zach be when his endurance fails him? Who will he be with? What will happen as a result?

I don't like any of the answers my mind conjures, flashes of unfamiliar faces in dank and dirty places, from which there may be no escape.

No, I hear myself silently object, *I won't allow it. I won't lose him to a fate like that!*

I reflect on something Zach said to me on, basically, the same subject: *What if God's will is for me to go out there and do what I can? And what if, in the name of fear or laziness, I allow myself to believe that is contentedness...?*

I finish his thought. ... *I do nothing. Living in doubt, I'll hate myself forever.*

But Zach had also asked for a sign, some undeniable show of faith, that staying here in Lancaster is what God wants for him, that this is where he truly belongs.

Then I put two and two together, and come up with the only reasonable answer, the sum of all these troubling parts. The question that remains isn't whether I should finally take that fateful step, and offer my body to Zach, at long last.

But.... *How?*

VOLUME TWO

CHAPTER 5

Zach and I decide to take the bus to the library. This is how I came before, so I know the bus we need. And, we both agree, that if Zach is going to be living the Englischer lifestyle, he may as well start now.

The library isn't huge, but it's recently been refurbished and it's quite nice. Beside the posters for teen thrillers, or cartoon characters with slogans like *Reading is Feeding ... Your Brain,* the library is very modest and sedate: clean lines, brown carpet, shelves of books, rows of computer monitors.

Zach and I take a look at the catalogue on the library computer data bank. As Amish, we're still allowed to use these things from time to time, but we choose not to have them in our homes. Cars, for example: we can ride in them if we must, but that's not the same as driving one, much less owning one.

But it's hard to get a feel for much on the computer, so we start strolling around. The litany of book titles blurring past is truly dizzying, nearly breathtaking. *It's true,* I think to myself, *there really are more books here than any person could read in a lifetime, about any subject one could want to learn about.*

I'm impressed by the staggering wealth of thought that sits on these shelves. I think about all the time each book took to write, to research, to rewrite, and edit. And for every book, the hours pile up in my brain with a staggering quantity; it's more than I can think about.

But I do start to wonder what I'm missing in all these books. *Surely,* I think to myself, *this can't simply be book after book of lies and war dates. The human experience is filled with a lot more than that, just like Zach said. And here's proof: row after row of poetry, philosophy, math, the sciences, the humanities, history, and humor, from the darkest of man's dreams to the summit of his ambitions.*

I begin to wonder if my life would change were I to pick up one of these books, any one of them, completely at random, opened that book up to any page, and read that page all the way through. *Would there be some nugget of wisdom I might remember for the rest of my life,* I ask myself, *something I could take away and remember, share with others as they need it? Is it possible, that just one page from just one book could change my whole world view, alert me to things I'd never considered, or even thought to consider?*

Would I want my life to change that way?

If I knew for certain that reading any one page from any book would change my life, without knowing if that change would be for the better or the worse, would I do it?

I cannot find the answer.

So I look to Zach, who started asking long before I did. I see his eyes combing over the spines, taking in the titles, the authors' names; perhaps imagining his own name among them someday.

After a few quiet minutes, we exit the library, and stroll around the little landscaped area between the building and the parking lot, finally taking a seat on the concrete bench under the awning.

"Well," I say. "What do you think?"

Zach chuckles a bit as he looks around. "Katie, it's great, and you're sweet. But you know it's not the same."

"It's the same knowledge, the same facts, the same poetry, and all that."

"Katie, you remember when we talked about education and experience?" Reading my nod, he says, "I'm looking for both, Katie. Do you understand?"

"You can always enroll at Lehigh University; that's not too far. What kind of classes do you think you'd take?"

Zach looks at me, wincing in uncertainty. "Are you making fun of me?"

"Zach, no! I'm trying to help you figure this out. Now c'mon, what classes?"

"I can't go to college yet," Zach said. "I have to complete high school first. I'll have to do a GED program."

My face heats. Of course, he'll need more than the eighth grade education that we all receive, but isn't their high school another four years? And then more school? With a sinking stomach, I ask, "How long will the GED program take?"

"I don't know. I'll have to take a test, classes, and study."

"And then college?"

"Ja."

"It seems like a lot."

Zach sighs. "Ja, Katie, I'm sorry. I shouldn't have snapped at you like that. It's just, I think about this, and my head starts spinning..."

"I know," I say, rubbing his back, leaning against his shoulder as he rubs his forehead with his thumb and index finger. "It's okay, Zach. We're gonna work this out, don't you worry." Zach puts his arm around me and pulls me in, giving me a big hug and a soft kiss, followed by a loving nuzzle.

But I know the truth, the words Zach can't seem to

understand or to say; for Zach, it's not about going to college, as much as it is leaving Faith's Landing.

And leaving us.

**

Katie's mamm, Mary, wanders out to the field behind the house, where the barn has stood since before Katie was born. One hundred feet by two hundred feet of rotting Douglas fir planks and beams, the "old girl" as her daed, Daniel Lapp, calls it, seems as spongy and gray as the clouds that are thickening above it. Daniel walks slow circles around the barn, peering at details and shaking his head, as Mary approaches from the house.

"How's she holding up?" Mary asks.

"I dunno," Daniel replies, hands on his waist, still slender for his more than fifty years. His age shows in his graying brown hair and the thickening creases on his face, much more so than in his torso, which is more muscular than those of a lot of men who are half his age. Amish are ranchers, farmers, blacksmiths, factory workers, and furniture makers. Say what you will, but Amish life makes you strong.

But not strong enough to control the weather.

Daniel says, "She may hold up, but I'm worried about that sky."

Mamm looks up, past his broad shoulders, to the thickening clouds. "They say it's going to rain after not too long; shouldn't be too bad."

Daniel looks back at the rotting barn. "Hope so. There's no time to put up a new barn before it rains. But I don't like the idea of leaving a hazard up; could do some terrible damage."

"Worst it'll do is come down. Things get bad, and we can move the mares across the lane, to the McCormick's' place."

Daniel considers, then looks deeper into his wife's eyes. "You seem worried, but it's obviously not about the barn." After waiting for Mamm to volunteer it, Daniel finally asks, "What is it, Mary?"

Mary wrestles with her responsibility to her daughter's privacy on the one hand, and, on the other, her responsibility to Katie's long-term well-being.

Trapped.

But one thing she can't do, and has never been able to do, is lie: not to her husband, not to her children, and not to her God. Mary adheres to set policy in this regard: *speak the truth or say nothing at all.*

Mary doesn't always speak. But this time, Daniel doesn't give her any choice. She says, "It's Katie, Daniel."

"Katie? What's wrong with our daughter?"

Mary stammers a bit. "Well, it's not Katie herself, actually —"

"It's her boyfriend, Zach."

"Yes, Daniel."

"Things aren't just settling down there, as you'd hoped."

"We *both* did."

"Then neither one of us should be surprised," Daniel says, patience seeping away from his tone at an alarming rate. "What's happening there now? She's not going to run off with him?"

"Um, no, not that I know of..." It's as if it's more than Mary can put into words; concepts that are too terrible for her to consider, or even describe.

"What *do* you know of, Mary?"

"Well, Daniel, she's worried that Zach is going to be leaving, sooner rather than later." Mary keeps glancing down at the ground, at her fidgeting fingertips, anywhere but up into her husband's eyes. She knows how he's going to react. She doesn't even want to tell him, but she knows that she doesn't have a choice. She goes on to say, "Katie's beginning to think that, well, that she might be, um, uniquely qualified to entice him not to go."

Daniel gives it a little thought, the answer to the riddle his wife is so clumsily trying to say, finally coming together in his mind. "Oh no, she isn't going to —?"

"Well now, Daniel, she didn't say that exactly. I might be

getting a little ahead of myself —"

"Better that, than to be two steps behind."

Mary holds her hands out to calm him, her words coming faster. "Daniel, stay calm —"

"Stay calm? Mary, our daughter's about to make of herself a concubine, a harlot, for the sake of some childhood crush?"

"It's not just a crush," Mary says. "She really does love him. They're going to be married, I think —"

"Then you're in favor of this?!"

"No, Daniel, of course not." Wind ripples over the tips of the tall grass, flipping up the collar of Daniel's work shirt, and pushing back the flap of Mary's bonnet. "We have to do something, of course. But if we're not careful, we could lose her trust —"

"Better that, than Katie losing her —"

"We have to tread lightly, Daniel."

"The way the Yoders have been with Zachariah? Look at how much good that's done for them, or for him!" After a moment of consideration, thoughts swirling in his mind, Daniel smiles vaguely at the first few drops of an ad hoc idea. "Maybe it's time I had a little chat with John, see what his thoughts are."

Mary looks on, her mouth twisting in a worried wriggle.

"You will be careful though, Daniel. Whatever you men do, make sure you don't just scare our children into the hills, and we never see either of them again. Daniel, I can't lose my baby —!"

"All right, Mary, all right," Daniel says, resting his mighty hand on her tiny shoulder. "Don't worry. We'll take care of everything."

'I'm sure you will,' Mary thinks to herself, *'that's what worries me.'*

CHAPTER 6

I bump into Zach the next day, which is an unexpected treat. At least, it starts out that way. I've taken the horse and buggy into town to pick some of the sundries we need, things we can't grow or sew for ourselves. Some of these are personal items related to hygiene. Nothing too exotic, but nothing I'd want to go on and on about either. So I happen to bump into Zach in the market, where he is carrying a red plastic shopping basket filled with fruit juices, boxes of Triscuits and Ritz crackers, and several blocks of cheddar and jack cheeses.

We share a few moments of pleasant surprise and small talk. He seems more upbeat than he's been, a little ray of sunshine poking up beneath the low-lying cloud cover. I glance down at the stuff in his basket. "Having another rumspringa party tonight?"

He looks at the basket too, then offers up a little chuckle in recognition; cheese and crackers, fruit juice to mix the cocktails. He says, "I guess all that's missing is a dance mix CD." We share a chuckle.

"Hey, maybe that's the sign you're looking for," I say, with a slightly forced chuckle. I'm only half-joking, after all.

"Sign?"

"That you really do belong here in Lancaster. This is where the parties are, right?" I chuckle a bit more, but I let it dribble away, like the weak and ineffectual ploy that it is.

'Why don't you ask me to the party?' I want to say, so I think it at him, hoping it'll somehow sink in. *'I'll show you how much fun staying in Faith's Landing can be!'*

But Zach says, "It's really more of a get-together. A buddy of mine is filling out college forms. Not much of a party, but if he gets into University of Missouri, and gets the scholarship he wants, he says I can move with him."

"Missouri?" I feel like I've been punched in the stomach, which, I hope, doesn't show. As casually as I can, I say, "Oh, I see. That does sound ... interesting."

Obviously, my expression has given away some measure of my horror at the thought of Zach moving so far away. "It's not decided yet," Zach says. "Just an idea."

'Oh God,' I nearly cry out. *'Please don't let his friend get a scholarship!'* But what I say is, "Oh, Zach, it sounds like a great opportunity for your friend...and a good opportunity...."

Zach smiles, with a warmth I've come to relish, but which now only feels like a cold blade sinking into my heart. We walk together to the register, pay for our wares, and then exit the store together, side by side. Once again, I find my mind wandering, to a reality where we are married, doing the shopping together, taking our groceries back to our home, our children.

But it's not reality.

Not yet.

I have to shake my head clear of those happy thoughts. *'Forget that fantasy, Katie,'* I urge myself. *'Get on the ball and make a move, or a fantasy is all that's ever going to be!'*

"I'll see you to your buggy," Zach says, always the gentleman. We share a bit more small talk on the way. Zach mentions the weather, and I try to stay away from anything that makes Lancaster look bad.

When we get to my buggy, I "accidentally" slip, and let my bags of groceries fall to the ground. Since everything in them is either in a plastic bottle or cardboard box, I know nothing will break. And it is an irresistible opportunity for us to kneel together and collect the things, putting them back into the bag. It's a moment for me to "allow" my skirt to show a little curve of my calf.

I roll my shoulder a bit as I collect the shampoo, the toothpaste; smiling and giggling the way I know boys like.

"I'm so clumsy these days," I say, "I just don't know what the matter could be; so tense." Our faces are quite close, and I can feel his eyes falling to my lips, so close to his own. I go on to say, in what I imagine is a sultry whisper, "I wish there was some way I could ... relieve some of this ... this pressure."

We kneel next to the buggy, locked in this moment, between the years of building tension behind us and the gaping voluminous years to come. But all those countless seconds fade in comparison to this moment, these few seconds, when our lips are so close, and getting closer still, until they finally reconnect in a subtle and sublime union.

We've kissed before, as I've said. But we don't do it often, and when we do, it reminds me of everything I've ever known, confirms everything I've ever thought, illustrates everything I've ever dreamed. It feels like it's going to go on forever, and I wish it would, but for all the other things our lives together will bring, which cannot begin until this kiss ends. So it is with bittersweet regret that I pull away, our lips parting, and we both must say goodbye to that moment forever.

But I hope and pray for more just like it, even better.

We hover near to one another, our faces still close, and our souls ever closer. He clears his throat, and says, "Well, um, I better get going. My buddy Dylan's expecting me around two this afternoon. He thinks it'll take hours to fill all out all those forms."

I break a little smile, half in reflection of our lovely kiss, half in recognition of its poignant pointlessness.

I'll have to do better next time.

***

Zach takes his own buggy to nearby Easton, where his Englischer friend, Dylan Fisher, lives in his parent's basement. Zach and Dylan became friends during Zach's rumspringa parties when Zach helped Dylan home after a night of too much drinking. Since then, they've had each other's backs.

So Dylan listens patiently to Zach as they chat, between filling out lines of information on Dylan's admissions applications and financial aid forms.

"She said you belong in Lancaster?" Dylan says, popping an Oreo cookie into his mouth. "Isn't that for you to say?"

"Well, ultimately it is, I suppose. Or ... God?"

"You say that like a question," Dylan says. "If you believe in God —"

"Of course I do, yes, absolutely I do."

"Then why the question?"

Zach thinks about it a bit, shrugging his confusion. "Well, I ... I believe in God, but that doesn't mean I quite understand what He wants or expects of me. I used to know. That is, I never really wondered."

"You just figured you'd stay."

"Yeah, sure. I mean, why not? Life for an Amish kid is great! It's all coloring and spelling and storybooks, sports and races in the backyard."

Dylan offers up a nasty little chuckle. "Then they stick a rake in your hands and tell you to get to work."

"Exactly." A skeptical moment passes, before Zach has to correct himself with, "Well no, not exactly. There is work to be done, but I mean, you did chores after a certain age, didn't you?"

Dylan nods. "Sure, but I stayed in school. It's just different, Zach; there's no getting around it. Pity you can't have it both ways." Dylan reads Zach's expression: confused intrigue. Dylan explains, "It doesn't sound so much like you're dying to get out of Lancaster, just that you want more than it has to offer. That sound about right?"

"About right, I guess."

"Close counts," Dylan says, leaning back in his chair, hands behind his head. He stretches, his lean torso bending backward, suggesting an even greater height than his natural six foot stature. "So, what if you could stay in Lancaster and still get the education you want? At least you wouldn't have to sacrifice your relationship with Katie."

"I thought you wanted me to go with you to Missouri? The El-Dude Brothers, big men on campus!"

Dylan smiles, setting down his pen. "I would like that,

Zach. I'd like it a lot. And to tell you the truth, I think you'd kill at Columbia. But only if you're into it, only if you want to be there. If you go and spend the whole time moping about Katie, thinking about the folks back home, well, what would be the point of going?" After a caring pause, Dylan shakes Zach's shoulder a bit, and adds, "I want you to be happy, buddy. Maybe if you just sit on the fence instead of choosing either side —"

"Dylan, if it were that easy, I'd have thought of it a long time ago. I have to make a decision, and soon. Katie isn't leaving, and even if I stay in the area and study for my GED, I won't be able to marry her without taking my *Kneeling Vow*, at which point I'll be expected to live as an Amish man. If I stay, and we continue as we've been, in an unending courtship, it will only be cruel for her. She won't be able to marry me, and she won't have the freedom to love another." Zach takes a breath, his heart clenching at the thought of Katie in another man's arms.

"So, you want to leave her then?"

"I don't want to leave her."

"You should have another beer." Dylan said, averting his eyes.

"What?"

"It is your *rumdrinka*."

"Rumspringa, Dylan, you know it's pronounced

rumspringa."

"Why do you have to decide so soon though? Can't you extend your *rumspringa?*" Dylan says, over-pronouncing the word with a heavily affected German accent. "There's no limit to it, is there?" Zach can only shake his head, as Dylan goes on to suggest, "So get your education, then come back and settle in Lancaster, take your Kneeling Vow."

"You know *Kneeling Vow,* but not *rumspringa?*"

"Rumdrinka is funnier. C'mon, Zach, you haven't been Amish so long that you've lost your sense of humor?"

"I've always been Amish, and we don't lack for a sense of humor; that's an unfair stereotype." After a self-knowing moment that even Zach cannot deny, he adds, "We just don't believe in laughter." Both he and Dylan crack up at this, unfair stereotype though it may be.

In the echo of their mirth, silent confusion returns to fill the basement around them. "Seriously, though," Dylan says, "where do you think you belong?"

"How am I supposed to know that? I've only ever been one place my entire life. I don't have anything to compare it too!"

Dylan picks up his pen and hands it to Zach. "Then you better get to work."

***

The same evening, both Zach's daed, John Yoder, and Katie's daed, Daniel Lapp, attend a meeting of the community elders. The elders worked through community business: discussing the plans for our next quilt auction, concerns about the integrity of our rotting barn, and Daniel's hope that the community will help build a new one, sooner, rather than later. After the meeting at the Hershberger house, Daniel pulls John aside for a private chat, just outside on the porch.

"What's the panic, Daniel?" John asks, only half-joking. "We'll take care of the barn, soon as this storm comes and goes."

"It's not that, John, although I do appreciate it."

"We look out for each other around here, eh? Not like out there, among the Englischers —"

"Actually, John, that's what I want to talk to you about ... sort of."

Ignoring the crickets, and unable to see the round, bright moon or the uncountable stars lurking high above the clouds, John looks at Daniel with a new seriousness. "It's the kids?"

"Precisely. John, I'm afraid my Katie may be trying to seduce your boy Zach."

"Seduce? That's a rather coarse term, Daniel. They've been courting for a while now; I hardly think that —"

"It's not just courting, John! Katie's afraid that Zach is

making plans to leave Lancaster."

"He may be."

"And she seems ready to do whatever it takes to change his mind. *Whatever it takes, John!*"

Silence returns, punctuated by the crickets and the muffled muttering of the elders still inside the house. John gives it a little thought; no more is required.

"Well, that won't do," John says.

"It most certainly will not," Daniel agrees.

"It's nothing against your Katie, of course. She's a fine girl, Daniel."

"And your son will make an excellent husband, I haven't a doubt." Daniel lets a nervous moment pass before adding, "If only he'd manage to take a stand."

"He's finding his ground. We all do it at one time or another."

"Yes, John. But for how long a time?" Their words come quicker, their voices louder. But they hush themselves, keenly aware that this is not a conversation either of them wants overheard. Daniel adds, "If something doesn't change soon, our situation will only get worse."

"What would you have me do? I've tried to get him to take the Kneeling Vow. He's just not ready. I'm thinking of other ways I can curtail his freedoms in the meantime, but too much of that will send him running into the Englischers' arms, just as sure as we're standing here."

"If that's God's will," Daniel says, "so be it. At least he won't disgrace my daughter."

A long moment crawls by, in which John reconsiders his welcome of Daniel's concerns. "What your daughter does or doesn't do is no fault of my boy's, Daniel. If you can't control her, that's your problem. If she can't control herself —"

Daniel sticks an angry finger into John's face, but John swats it away quickly, angrily. "Don't you dare cast aspersions on my daughter!" Daniel shouts. "That son of yours doesn't know what's good for him; that's fine. But I'm the one who decides what's good for my daughter, and I don't think that includes seeing any more of your son!"

"Try to drive a wedge between them, and you're guaranteeing that they'll wind up together, probably a good while before their wedding. And then, as you said yourself, all our situations will be a whole lot worse."

John asks, "What do you suggest then?"

"I suggest you lower your tone of voice when addressing me. I suggest you not make any demands to which you have no right."

"I have every right! She's my daughter."

"Daniel, you're acting like a fool! The only way out of this is to be calm, to think through it; perhaps a bit of prayer."

"You would sit back and do nothing?"

"On the contrary, Daniel, I will do whatever it takes. But forbidding them from seeing each other is not the way."

The two men stare each other down, the dark night expansive around them, hiding the clouds behind its ink curtain. There is only silent tension between them, until Daniel spits out, "We'll see about that!"

CHAPTER 7

My daed comes home that night, bursting through the front door, with more negative energy than I've ever seen in him. We Amish pride ourselves on our self-control, our restraint; but we're still human, just people, after all. And when a man feels that his daughter's been insulted, and worries that her life is at a terrible crossroads, that's when a man's ire gets up.

"Katie," he calls to me from across the house, "Katie, wake up and get down here!" I haven't fallen asleep yet, which is just as well.

I don't have much choice but to come downstairs and face my daed, to hear whatever he has to say. My mamm comes out of her room as well, standing between us, with the same look of fear and confusion I believe myself to be wearing.

That's certainly how I'm feeling.

He says, "You're not to see that boy anymore, Zachariah

Yoder."

"What? Daed, why —?"

"You know very well why, young lady. That boy's corrosive influence is having a terrible effect on you." I don't say anything, but Mamm and I exchange a worried glance, each telling the other the same thing.

He knows.

But what's racing through my mind now is, '*How does he know?*' I'm still looking at my Mamm, and her expression betrays her. Her mouth is a little frown, eyebrows arching, forehead creasing in impotent worry and regret. I'm hurt; angry at her betrayal. But there's no time to deal with her, to ask her why she would share my secrets with the one man who shouldn't know them, to ask her how I should ever trust her again with my secrets, or even my friendship.

Because Daed is still yelling at me.

Not yet.

Esther steps down the stairs, silently rubbing the sleep from her eyes. Mamm rushes to her and ushers her quickly back up and into the room, closing the door behind them.

Daed turns to me. "This is a disgrace, an infamy! 'We are put to shame, for we have heard reproach; dishonor has covered our face, for foreigners have come into the holy places of the Lord's house.'"

Daed's bellow of Jeremiah 51:51 fills the room, and even the small, silent voice within me must quiet up and show some respect. This is no mere scolding, because what I did was no mere transgression.

'Wait a minute,' I have to remind myself, *'I haven't done anything! Mamm only assumed that I might do something! Sure, she was right, and I still might, but Daed doesn't know that!'*

"I thought you mature enough to handle this kind of relationship, but now I can see I've given you too much credit, and far too much freedom. Look what that's done for Zach: he's becoming unhinged, and he's dragging you down with him, straight into the fire!"

The Abyss? He's just going off to college; he may not even go! But I can only think these things, because to say them would earn a terrible rebuke. And it would be disrespectful. My daed loves me, and this flash of temper is born of that love, and the care he's always shown for me. I don't like what he's saying, but I'd never demean his right to say it. And in truth, I'd be hurt were he to show no interest at all.

Mamm steps out of the girls' room and closes the door behind her once more, then comes down the stairs looking at us, with a hopeless hope that the worst won't come to pass, even as it does before our very eyes.

"So let him go," Daed goes on. "We'll find you a more suitable young man."

You'll find me a suitable young man? Like buying a new plow horse? Love doesn't work that way, and you know that. But love isn't your concern, is it? And I do love him, Daed, I do...

Daed says, "We'll be able to hold our heads up in the community again, not have to go on ignoring being stared at and talked about."

That's what you really care about, I want to say, *your social standing, your precious community. Zach's right: we are all so insulated. It's great to have a community, but when that's all you care about, that's all you wind up with. When you care more about them than you do for the happiness of your own daughter, there's something seriously wrong.*

"I know it's not what you want to hear," Daed says, "but it's my decision, and I'll have no argument."

Your decision? It's your decision? Daed, it's my life! My rumspringa! Am I to go on living as your puppet, your pet, your plaything? Don't I get a chance to decide how my life will be, whom I will love and marry, when and where and how? It's your decision? Your decision?

Then my throat finally takes over, in a voice so low and cool that it fills the room, even at such a low volume, even with the utterance of a single, tiny word.

"No."

Shock echoes around us; Daniel looking from me to my

mamm, who steps toward me and puts her arm around my shoulder. She's being protective of me, and I'm grateful for it. My daed's face reads complete disbelief, anger twisting his face until it is almost unrecognizable.

"What did you say to me, young la —?"

"I said no, Daed." A little moment slips by between us. He's ready to hear me explain. And it'd better be good. I add, "I love you, and I won't disrespect you ... but I won't simply obey you like a dog, not when it comes to this."

"Not when it — Katie, this is when it matters, this is when you need to listen to me, trust me — "

"No, Daed, this is when you need to listen to me! I love Zach, and you know that. And nothing's going to change it. He's going through a time of trial, and I'm going to see it through with him. And if I can keep him here, I will."

We stand with our eyes locked, chins jutting, our wills pitted against each other's. Mamm stands between us, her loyalty torn, her personal feelings all but shredded by the conflicting forces at work on her from every angle. She respects my position, but fears for my future; she loves her husband, but worries for our relationship; she loves God, but fears that our hardening hearts won't allow God's best plans for us to come to fruition. She's afraid her household is being ripped apart.

Because it is.

In that horrendous silence, that heaving stillness around us, Daed's own voice drops down, low, gravelly, and potent.

From behind a sneer that pains him as much as it expresses his pain, Daed looks me dead in the eye, and says, "Get out."

"Daniel, no —"

"I won't have this kind of affront in my own home, from my own daughter! I've made my decision, and I won't abide open defiance!"

"You'd prefer I defied you in secret?"

He points a furious finger toward the door. "That's it! Out! Get out this instant!"

"Daniel, she's in her bathrobe," Mamm says, her voice cracking and pleading, "it's freezing outside, there's a storm coming —"

"There's a storm coming all right," Daed says. He knows she's right; he can't toss me out into the cold night. But he can't back down either, or whatever power he still holds as man of the house, and head of the household, will be lost.

To his daughter.

And I know he won't abide that either.

So he makes the only choice he can, and it sinks in my gut like a cold stone tossed into a muddy pond.

"You can stay the night," he says. "In the morning, pack

your things, and get out." With that, he leaves us to our sudden silence.

My body begins to tremble, as my mamm wraps her arms around me and pulls me close. Sweat gathers on my back; despite the cold, my heart starts to pound behind my ribs, my mouth goes dry as tears well up behind my eyes and make their sorrowful escape down my cheeks. My sniffling grows into a sob before I can control it, and once it starts it only continues, building strength, drawing the air from my lungs.

The warm feel of my mamm's arms around me fills me with nostalgia for my childhood, for those loving nights and sunny days of youth that I know will never come again.

Not for me.

Mamm whispers soft words into my ear, tender reassurances that it will be okay, that this wrong will be righted by prayer, by faith.

But as the Bible says in James 2:26: "But I know that faith alone won't do it. For, as the body without the spirit is dead, so faith without works is dead also."

What's going to be required to save us all now is not merely faith.

But deed.

CHAPTER 8

The day begins with the click of my doorknob and the creaking of the hinges. Daed stands on the other side, his face a grim visage. Outside, rain pours down in sheets, the rattling percussion of a billion tiny wet thuds on the roof, telling me that the storm has finally come.

And one look into my Daed's cold face tells me the same thing. Without a word, he steps away, leaving the door open.

I pack my clothes and the few personal possessions I own: my Bible, a gift from my grandmother the year before she died; and a small framed photo of me and my folks when I was just a little girl, barely out of diapers. I pack my things, along with a toothbrush and a few related necessities, into a floral-patterned suitcase, and carry it across the room. I look around at my bedroom, one last glance at my childhood, before turning and walking away, to leave it behind forever.

I walk down the stairs and step into the living room, my

mamm standing in silence. She's been crying all night; I can tell by the redness of her cheeks, the swollen bags around her eyes.

Esther looks up at our mamm, her little voice soft and sad. "Where's Katie going, Mamm?"

Mamm looks at our daed, her expression silently begging him to relent.

He looks at me: his mouth a stern slit, his eyes cold and determined. I look back, hoping to reflect some of that same determination. Already standing by the front door, he pulls it open, and stands there, grim-faced.

But he doesn't see what we see, and our sudden smiles draw Daed's attention to the man standing on the other side of the doorway.

Zach stands there with his hand up, knuckles out, ready to knock. He wears a look of mild surprise for his knock to be preempted, but it's quickly replaced by the look of concern for what's gathered us all at the door, suitcase in my hand.

"Zach!"

"Katie, what's going on?"

My daed looks Zach up and down, the rain pouring behind him. "What're you doing here?"

He looks my daed up and down in a similar fashion. "I came here to speak with you."

Lightning cracks outside, thunder rolling as the rain comes down even harder. Zach's horse is soaked to the skin, trying in vain to shake its mane dry. My daed says, "See to your mare; barn's around back."

It's as much invitation as Zach's going to be extended; then Daed closes the front door, to leave us all standing in the awkwardness of Zach's exit. Without looking at her, Daed says to Mamm, "I didn't hear you go out to the phone shed this morning, Mary."

Mamm just clears her throat, hands fidgeting. "I thought he should hear it from you."

"You're trying to humiliate me!" Daed's rising voice shatters the awkward silence, shards so sharp they threaten to cut right through me, and, for the first time, my Mamm. "How dare you? Don't I have a right to say what goes on in my own home, of who comes and who goes? Must I be forced to explain myself to strangers, children no less!"

"He's not a stranger," I say, calm but without fear, having already lost it all. "And he's not a child."

"This much, I know," Daed says, looking back at my Mamm. "Take the girls into their room, they can play with their dolls there, for now."

Mamm nods and crosses to the girls, taking each by the hand and leading them away. Daed and I look at each other from across the room. It may as well be from across the entire state of Pennsylvania.

Zach's knocks return to the front door. My daed lets him in, very formally, closing the door behind him.

After a moment of brief disquiet, Daed says, "You came all the way here, in this downpour; must have been for a good reason."

Zach nods, clearing his throat. "Yes sir, it is." Zach looks at me, and I can't help but smile at him. I'm so grateful that he's come to me in my time of crisis. It proves what I've always known, reaffirming what I've always believed.

Not giving Zach a fair chance, Daed barks, "Out with it, boy. Speak your peace."

"Well, sir, I understand there's some kind of misunderstanding here, and I want to try to clear it up."

"I understand everything perfectly well," he says, glaring at me.

"But I don't think you do, sir. First of all, let me just say that Katie has done nothing, and I mean *nothing*, to compromise your family name or bring any shame at all upon this house; nothing even close."

Daed stares back at him, as Mamm walks down the stairs to re-enter the room.

Zach goes on to say, "She's been a good example, urging me to do the right things, and for the right reasons: to pray, to take my time, and not rush into anything drastic. You should be proud of her, rewarding her for her excellence, not throwing her out of her home."

"What business is it of yours?"

"Because I am the cause of this misunderstanding, Mr. Lapp. I'll take whatever responsibility there is to bear in this mess. But no blame should fall to Katie; that's simply unfair."

Daed takes a single, threatening step toward Zach, who does not step backward. "And what part did you play in this mess?"

A nervous smile twitches on Zach's face, as the thunder rolls outside, rain hitting the roof louder, faster. "That's something I was hoping you could tell me. I haven't brought Katie to any of my rumspringa activities —"

"Activities," Daed repeats, disgust heavy in his tone. "Cavorting, imbibing, bacchanalia!"

"And she never expressed an interest," Zach goes on. "But I know you were a young man once —"

"All the more reason for me not to trust you. Not all young men are as considerate of their intended as I was."

"And it shows in Katie's upright behavior," Zach counters. "And all I've done is what every other young Amish man and a lot of young Amish women do —"

"Harlots," my daed says, "strumpets." The words vibrate

in a cold chill along my bones. When the thunder claps nearby, my body jolts in surprise, in fear.

"But not Katie," Zach says, calmly making his point. The angrier my daed seems, the calmer Zach is in response, and it's a balance that is sure to tip in Zach's favor. "If you can't trust me, I understand that. But surely you can trust your daughter. Look in your heart; you'll know I'm right. You know she's pure, and good, and decent, and honest ..."

My daed just looks at me, his sneer melting away.

"You know she is where God wants her to be," Zach goes on, "in the bosom of her family."

Daed nods, his head moving with great subtlety, even his blink a more visible response.

Zach adds, "This is where she belongs now."

Then Daed pushes a breathy, almost inaudible, "Yes."

"And this is where you want her to remain."

"Yes."

Zach smiles and steps back, his own eyelids blinking in a calm resolution. My suitcase finally drops from my hands, and I take two steps toward Daed. He meets me halfway. We hug in the center of the living room, the storm grinding away outside, roaring its frustration like a wild beast, unable to deliver the killing blow to its wounded prey.

'Not yet,' I think to myself, as I fall into my daed's arms, his chest big and strong in front of me, his arms lovingly squeezing, hands pressing against my back, the side of his face against my cheek.

Mamm picks up my suitcase and carries it toward my bedroom, saying to Zach, "You'll stay for breakfast, of course."

Zach looks at me, then at my daed, taking in our happy reunion. He looks back at my mamm with a humble smile. "I don't want to intrude."

"Nonsense," Daed says, extending his hand in friendship. "We insist."

Zach nods and shakes my daed's hand: strong, confident. "I'd like that, Mr. Lapp. Thank you."

The day passes with almost idyllic splendor. The breakfast casserole is hot and tasty, bacon and sausage and eggs and cheese, baked until a crispy crust forms along the top. The corn biscuits and butter, and the baked oatmeal go so well together, you'd think they were Adam and Eve's first breakfast foods.

Such a feeling of hominess surrounds us in our repast, it strikes me how different things were only a while before, when my family was coming apart at the seams. I look at Zach as Esther holds his attention, treating her with every bit as much respect and consideration as he's always shown to me.

I realize, *'He's the reason we're all still together, enjoying this meal. And how calm he seems, so at home; not the frenzied, nervous young man who can't find his way.*

Why can't I make him see this for himself?'

Later, he and my daed trudge out in the rain to check on the barn, circling around it and spending almost an hour overlooking the interior details. When they come back, both men agree that the barn should come down, as soon as the rains pass. Daed treats Zach with much more respect now, respect that Zach has earned. I even see Daed smile at Zach once or twice.

As Mamm and I and the girls prepare dinner (the girls contribute a bit less), Zach and my daed carry on a colorful conversation in the living room, about the Bible. Should every word be taken as literal fact, or some as myth and some as history? Was Judas chosen by Jesus to betray him, or did Jesus simply know this would happen? Did Paul really travel with a woman called Thecla, who baptized herself in a pool of sharks?

Their tempers never flare as these ideas pass between them, and this brings me considerable relief. Things are going so well; everybody is getting along just wonderfully, and the last thing we need is for a heated religious debate to get out of hand and spoil things, as they so often do.

At dinner, I can barely take my eyes off Zach. He's so handsome, so manly, and so comfortable. I know this is where he belongs, with me, at a dinner table like this one, with a family like this one.

A family of our own.

The idea so thrills me that I can't rid my imagination of it, no matter how hard I try. And that thrill is all-encompassing, as my mind's eye envisions our meals, our days.

Our nights.

My body is flushed with heat, my skin alive with the sharp points of a million tiny needles, falling on me like raindrops. I can't deny the heat of my blood, the passion in my heart. This has been a long day, and every emotion has passed through me at its maximum: fear, desperation, relief, gratitude, and love.

Lust.

And struggle, though I do, to deny it or ignore it or resist it, I can no more do that than I can step out of my own body, discard my skin, and go about as a spirit among the living.

I'm not a spirit. I am among the living. And I've waited too long to start living: living the way adults do, the way men and women do all over the world.

'Why not here?' asks the echoing, disembodied voice that lives in the back of my mind. *'Why not us? Why not now?'*

Tonight.

'Isn't this what God wants?' I have to ask myself. *'If Zach is here, mustn't this be where God wants him to be? I'd taken this storm as an omen, but maybe I've been wrong all along; it's the instrument of God's will putting us together, giving us*

a chance to settle family differences, and unite under one roof.

To be as one.

And who am I to defy God's will? He's brought Daed and Zach together in friendship; He brought me and Daed back together as a family.

Surely, He is bringing me and Zach together, in love.' And, as certain as I am in God's desire for our union, as faithful as I am that no force can defy His mighty will, I also recall that faith without deed is dead. I have the faith.

Now, I must do the deed.

VOLUME THREE

CHAPTER 9

It's the strangest sensation, one I've never known before. I almost feel like I'm dreaming, or having what I've heard referred to, as an out-of-body experience. I can hardly believe it's happening at all.

Am I really getting up out of bed? Sure enough, my legs straighten beneath me, crossing each other as they carry me to the door. *I'm not really going to open that door though, am I?* But I do, the knob cold in my hand. *I'm not actually sneaking around to the basement door?*

'See for yourself,' I hear that voice say, as I step carefully, anxious that the creaking stairs will give me away.

The logic flows through me, reassuring me, quashing any doubts. *The rains never let up, and that's God's doing. The fact that Zach had to stay the night must also be God's will. And, if so, for what other possible reason that this?*

But that pesky little voice answers, *'To give you the opportunity not to do it, to resist the temptation.'*

'No,' I leap to correct myself, *'I've resisted temptation all this time. Surely God wouldn't keep trying me like that. If this is a test of anyone, it's of Zach, not me; a test of his desire for me, a test of his readiness to take me, a test of his readiness to leave me behind forever.'*

My heart is pounding as I reach the bottom stair of the basement, the cot set up in the corner. We have extra space upstairs, but both Zach and Daed insisted that the basement would be more appropriate. At first my thought was that Daed must have thought, *'Zach doesn't want to tempt me.'*

But as I see him on that cot, I realize Zach was looking ahead, to the possibilities of being together in a secluded room, where nobody could see or hear us.

'It's meant to be,' I hear that voice in my head admit. *'How can it be any other way?'*

I step closer to the cot, my heart beating faster still. When Zach turns, I feel as though it will finally just explode.

"Katie?"

"Zach." He reaches for the propane lamp on the table near the cot, but I stop him with, "No, don't! Leave the light off."

I take another step toward him, and Zach sits up, the sheets over his red long johns. "Katie —"

'Here it is,' I say to myself, *'the moment of truth! Everything we've ever been to each other, every hour we've spent making each other laugh, letting each other cry…it's all been leading to this.*

Finally…'

But the next voice I hear isn't Zach's.

It's Daed's. "What on Earth is going on down here?"

I turn and back up, finding myself standing next to Zach sitting on the cot, as Daed walks down the basement stairs, Mamm behind him, a deer rifle in front of him.

"Katie!" she says, with a disapproving tone. "How could you?"

I look around, not sure of what to say. There isn't much I *can* say, but to repeat the things I was thinking about: God's will, and the storm. But even as I think about it now, it makes less sense than before, when my body was doing the thinking, and my brain was just going along for the ride.

Daed says, "You little snit! I can't believe you lied to me, bald-faced, like the serpent himself."

I'd be quite offended to be compared to the devil himself, but I'm sad to observe that he's not too far off. I did try to tempt Adam with the apple, in this particular metaphor.

Zach stands and takes a step in front of me, a protective gesture that I appreciate. He says, "No, Mr. Lapp, you're wrong again! I was the one who lured Katie down here, during small talk after dinner. I was the serpent, not Katie. Yet, for the second time in a single day, you rush to judgment against your own. Mister Lapp, if you learn nothing today —"

"I'll rush to more than judgment, Mr. Yoder!" Daed raises the rifle and points it directly at Zach's face. "You've just admitted your guilt, there's not a jury on Earth's gonna convict me."

"Daniel, no!"

"Enough, Mary!" She recoils from behind him, terror in her eyes, the like of which I've never seen, certainly not on her pudgy face. Daed looks back at Zach. "Now pick up your clothes."

After an unsteady moment, Zach bends to his overalls. He opens them to step in, but Daed says, "Just pick 'em up. You can put them on outside."

I say, "Daed, it's still raining; he'll catch his death out there."

"Better out there than in here." He steps back, leaving a clear path to the steps leading up into the house. Zach crosses slowly toward the stairs, and I follow, but Daed glares at me. "Just the boy."

"Daed, no! I won't —"

"Just the boy!" Daed repeats, louder, angrier. Mamm crosses to me, holding me tight, both to offer comfort and to hold me back. So I stand there, clinging to her, as my daed leads Zach up the stairs. We stand in silence as the floorboards creak above us, the door opening and then slamming shut.

Zach is gone, and I'm certain I'll never see him again.

CHAPTER 10

Zach goes straight to Dylan's place. He's basically going from one family basement into another, but Dylan has become a trusted sounding board, and the source of some decent and fair-minded advice.

He also has plenty of dry clothes, and his mother's electric washer and dryer machine at the ready.

Zach arrives in the middle of the night. Dylan makes a pot of coffee and pours Zach a piping hot cup. "We have to keep it down," he whispers, "folks won't be up for a while yet." Dylan's father, a local pastor, doesn't keep farmer's hours.

Zach takes a sip of that hot coffee, the steam wafting up his nostrils, soothing and refreshing. Dylan says, "Rough night?" They share a chuckle, Zach sipping again as the laundry machine hums and tumbles nearby.

Zach tells Dylan everything.

Everything.

And then, he tells Dylan even more: "I tell you, it's a side of Katie I've never seen."

Dylan says, "I gotta tell ya, Zach, a lot of guys would swap their grannies to be in a basement with their girl like that. I really don't see why you're so upset."

"Because that's not Katie: not the Katie I've known all these years, not the Katie I fell in love with."

"So you are in love with her."

"I never said I wasn't."

"But you're willing to leave her behind?"

This stumps Zach, as he considers over a few more sips of hot coffee. Finally he says, "I'm afraid Daniel Lapp might be right."

"But, you just said you lied, took the heat because —"

"Not that, Dylan, I mean ... that I'm a bad influence on Katie, that I'm corrupting her. She never would have done that last year. Now? I dunno —"

Dylan taps Zach's shoulder, giving it a comforting little shake. "A year's a long time for a girl that age, Zach. Maybe she's got the bug, just like you. Maybe it's time you think about asking her to come with you."

Zach sits with the idea, as it sinks in. "Y'think?"

"Why not?"

It sinks in a bit further. "I dunno; I never thought about it. Katie's always been so into the idea of me reconsidering, staying here in Lancaster; she's so locked into her family, her sisters. They lost a brother, did I tell you that?" Dylan shakes his head. "Buggy accident, about four years ago. I don't think her daed ever got over it."

"Of course not," Dylan says. "Those kinds of things, you never get over completely. No wonder he's so protective of his daughter, eh?" Zach nods, seeing the old riddle in a new way. Dylan goes on, "Still, he can't keep her on the farm forever, can he? And if they're going their separate ways, it could be just as well that this is all happening. Maybe it's God's will that you both go away together, start your lives together someplace new. Think of what it could mean for Katie, a whole new world! This may be a shocker, Zach, but they let women into universities these days, too."

"Is that what you'll be majoring in, standup comedy?"

They both chuckle, but the laughter soon fades to serious contemplation, and a new and dangerous path for us all.

***

I am at a complete loss. Not only have I lost my love, Zach, but I've lost respect for my daed and my mamm both. I'm still upset she ever told Daed that I might be thinking about making a move on Zach. I never even told her that, but I did let her get a glimpse of it. *How could she betray me like that?* I've often asked myself since.

But I answer myself, with fatiguing regularity and unassailable logic: *She did it because she loves you, and cares about you, and considered it her duty as a parent; if not to secure your friendship, than at least to ensure your security, you ungrateful snit.*

So, I even turn away from my own counsel. Why shouldn't I? I never say the things I want to hear!

But I do pray, and, as often as not, I find myself asking God to make his will known to me, to make it clearer to me, so that even if I cannot be happy, then at least I will be at peace. But I know that along this way lies folly and blasphemy. "Do not be conformed to this world," Paul writes in Romans 12:2, "but be transformed by the renewal of your mind, that by testing you may discern what is the will of God, what is good and acceptable and perfect."

So I wait for a sign, the way Zach waits, and I wonder if we both aren't a sign for the other: pointing out the road we shall tread side by side, the course that God has mapped out for us. And I praise God for the signs I know will show themselves at the appointed time.

'Not yet,' I hear in the back of my mind, as if the clouds had been whispering the Lord's words into my ears the entire time. *'Not yet.'*

But what does it mean? I ask myself. *Is it joy or agony that is to come? How long a wait must I endure, can I endure?*

Thunder rolls nearby, the echo of a distant, unheard response. Despite the release of the showers last night, the storm has not drained. It is pausing now, to gather up more strength, absorb more of the shadows that create it, and that it creates; growing in the vacancy between then and now, between memory and imagination, between all that has ever come before, and all that will ever come after.

Trapped.

So I sit by a kerosene lantern, reading Jeremiah 9:23-24. *Thus says the Lord: "Let not the wise man boast in his wisdom, let not the mighty man boast in his might, let not the rich man boast in his riches, but let him who boasts, boast in this; that he understands and knows me, that I am the Lord who practices steadfast love, justice, and righteousness in the earth. For in these things I delight, declares the Lord."*

"Daughter," my daed says, as he steps into the room. I set the Bible down on my lap, closing it around the ribbon that will keep my place. Saint Paul and I still have much to contemplate. My daed goes on to say, "I know you're upset about what happened with Zach. I just want you to know that I don't blame you."

I sit without speaking, to show my respect and less obviously (I hope) to share my contempt.

He says, "Obviously, he tricked you into going down there.

He's older than you by a year, and all these thoughts in his head surely make this kind of chicanery more comfortable for him, more ... natural."

But he's wrong, of course, because Zach lied about being responsible, because going down to the basement was entirely my idea, and, out of my cowardice, I merely allowed Zach to step up and courageously take the blame. So I let my daed go on with his rambling and misguided speech, tracking the progress of the hole he digs for himself, even if he has no way of seeing it for himself, until he's buried in it.

He says, "And, after all, you're only a child, a mere sixteen-year-old." He spits out a contemptuous little chuckle, but I'm not sure who it's aimed at. When he adds, "And just a girl, at that!" he removes all doubt.

The hole gets deeper, but my amusement quickly runs thin.

"You can hardly be held accountable for your own actions, let alone almost anything a man does. I knew this all along; my own daed used to tell me, but I realize now that I lost sight of it somehow. I guess I was the one who was seduced by all this modern courting, the kissing, and the hayrides. It seems innocent enough, but so does letting a pony run loose in a meadow. Pretty soon, the horse has run off, and a pack of wolves has a tasty dinner."

It takes every ounce of my will to hold back a tirade on the hidden strengths of the human woman, modern or otherwise, that would make Joan of Arc proud. I'm ready to tell him that his own views, and their popularity in Amish communities, are among the reasons Zach wants to go to college, and among the better reasons, too.

But I don't. *'Why bother?'* I ask myself. *'If he thinks I'm no smarter than some wayward pony, to be corralled and worked and sold off to the highest bidder, he'll never understand me.'*

But I'm beginning to believe that *I* will, if I give myself a chance. *'In fact,'* I find myself thinking, *'there's a lot I could do, and a lot I could learn, if I give myself a chance...'*

Daed crosses to the door, and turns before leaving. "Glad we had this little talk, honey. I feel a lot better." Then he leaves.

I hear myself think, *'I'm glad one of us does,'* but, of course, I don't say it.

Not yet.

***

By the time Zach gets back to his family's home, Katie's daed has called Zach's father, John, and told him about what happened in Katie's basement. It wasn't a long conversation, but it didn't have to be.

Zach walked into a quiet gloom in his house. The kids were back in school, his mamm was standing by, knowing what was to come.

Dreading it.

John ushers Zach into the living room, and says, "I got a very troubling call from Daniel Lapp."

"Daed, I —"

"Don't you realize the kind of shame you've brought down on this house? As if it wasn't bad enough before, with your college talk, and your unending rumspringa —"

"Some people spend years —"

"And look what it's doing to you, doing to your life!" John shouts, his patience at an end, even beyond it. "You've ruined your relationship with Katie and her family, and you're sure not doing yourself any favors around here! I'm just glad your kid brother Isaac is around to provide a good example for the little ones."

Zach's mamm says, "John, give him a chance to explain —"

"Okay, yes, you're right, Ruth. I apologize." He turns to Zach. "I'm so concerned about doing everything I can, I forgot to give you the chance to do the same."

Zach can only stand there. To contradict Katie's daed's account would be to put her in danger. Zach wasn't going to do that in her basement, and he isn't about to do it in his father's living room.

And, getting no answer, John makes the predictable

assumptions, spitting out a disgusted breath and shaking his head. "How could you lure a sixteen-year-old into the basement of her father's home to seduce her, with her parents and little sisters in the house just above? What's gotten into your head, what's gotten into your heart?"

And Zach has no answer. He must let his father assume what he will, and, sadly, to act accordingly, as he sees fit.

"You've had too much freedom, you're not nearly man enough to handle it."

But here, Zach feels that he can speak without betraying me. "How can I become a man without the freedom to become one?"

"That won't be a problem." Zach stands, confused, as Isaac steps into the room. Mamm wraps her arms around Isaac's shoulder, and they wait to hear John explain. "I can't limit your freedoms, Zach, not really. I've puzzled and puzzled over it: punishments, and curfews, and extra chores, and the like. But I think we both know where things are headed. And now, with all this, I think it's better that we pull the trigger before you do any more damage to those around you, those you claim to love."

"Daed?" Isaac asks, "What are you saying?"

"You don't seem able to make this decision on your own," John goes on to tell Zach, and, by extension, the rest of the family. "So I'm making it for you."

Zach stands alone, his eyes finding his packed suitcase in the hall.

John recites from the Book of Luke in a cool, intimidating manner. "And he called the twelve together and gave them power and authority over all demons and to cure diseases, and he sent them out to proclaim the kingdom of God and to heal."

Ruth says, "John, are you sure you —?"

John goes on, "And he said to them, 'Take nothing for your journey; no staff, nor bag, nor bread, nor money; and do not have two tunics.'"

Even Zach asks, "Daed?"

"'And whatever house you enter, stay there,'" John continues, "'and from there depart. And wherever they do not receive you, when you leave that town, shake off the dust from your feet as a testimony against them.'"

Thick quiet settles in the room, as confusion becomes grim clarity.

John Yoder extends his hand to Zach, for what everybody in the room is certain will be the last time. "Good luck, Son."

Isaac protests, "Daed, no!"

"It's okay, Isaac," Zach says, forcing a smile. "I'll send word where you can find me. We'll stay in touch."

His mamm starts to cry, but John offers his son a final nod

and lets go of his hand. Zach pauses, as if waiting for words that he knows won't come. He sees himself in the position he rescued Katie from only the day before, and that very rescue has visited the same crisis upon his own head. He's assumed Katie's burden as his own, sacrificed his own family, that she might have her own. And he's done it willingly.

He kisses his mother on the cheek and wipes her tears, then turns and offers Isaac a hearty handshake that neither would forget. It's a reminder of their bond, of flesh and blood and birth that will traverse any distance and transcend any time.

Then, before any more words can be exchanged, Zach picks up his case and steps out the door of his family home.

CHAPTER 11

Zach takes his bag to Dylan's, who was happy to have him as a houseguest, and is even happier to help him work things out. Down in the basement, the two friends share a pepperoni pizza and a six-pack of root beer. But even though these are some of Zach's favorite foods, he can't enjoy them. He can't savor the seasoned pepperoni or the gooey melted cheese, so hot and nourishing. It can't nourish Zach, either. The sustenance he requires doesn't come in any cardboard box, and it doesn't come in thirty minutes or less, as Zach knows so terribly well.

"Don't be so glum, pal," Dylan says. "It's a good thing. Maybe the old man's right. You were waffling quite a bit."

"It's a big decision, Dylan. I've never done anything like this before. And once it's done, I can't undo it." Zach stares into an imagined distance, head shaking a bit. "Some mistakes, you spend your whole life paying for."

Dylan offers up a little chuckle, grabbing another piece of

pizza. "You need to look on the bright side, Zach; what's done is done. You've got the rest of your life to look forward to! And you don't have to worry, you're not alone. I'll be there with ya, the two of us, off to see the world, get an education, and finally start the lives we've been thinking about all this time."

"Yeah," Zach nods, "right. Well, it's not that, Dylan. I mean, I do think it's the right thing, going to college, leaving once and for all. But ... my family, y'know? You should have seen my daed's face. He wasn't mad; at least he wasn't showing it. It was more like ... more like a stranger's face than an angry father's face, like he'd already begun to forget me."

"Birdie's gotta leave the nest, Zach, and sometimes that requires a little push, right?"

"A shove is more like it."

"Six of one," Dylan says, reaching for a can of root beer, not needing to add: *half a dozen of the other.* '*I know what he means,*' Zach must admit, '*and he's probably right. My daed isn't thrilled with me right now, and he's making a difficult and painful choice. But it's as difficult and painful for him as it is for me. It doesn't mean he doesn't love me, it means that he does.*

And maybe this is just what I need: somebody to make the choice, push me off the fence, whichever side I land on. At least my feet will be on the ground.'

Dylan adds, "I bet if we called him right now, and he happened to be near enough to the phone shed out back to hear it, and answer — "

"Don't make fun, Dylan —"

"I'm just saying, if we could ask you father, right now, he'd say that he still loves you every bit as much as he ever did. And you'll be in touch with your kid brother, your mom. You'll see them all again, after a ... a period of adjustment."

Zach releases a worried sigh. "I hope so. You don't know how things work in the Amish world. We're very —"

"Stubborn?"

"Committed. It's part of what's kept us on the Earth for four hundred years. We adjust to things very, very slowly."

Dylan looks at Zach, wondering how much he should say, how much is too much. Finally, after a little chill he blames on the drafty basement, Dylan says, "You think you'll be able to adjust to not having her around?" Noting Zach's confusion, Dylan adds, "Katie."

Zach swallows hard and turns away. "I don't know."

***

It haunts me. *How could I be so wicked? First, to defy my father and to defy Zach, who was only here to speak on my behalf? Then to press myself upon him the way I did? It seemed reasonable at the time, but looking back, I'm embarrassed and ashamed. Mamm's right, it was an abuse of my power as a woman, an assault on Zach's lesser instincts, his weaker self.*

Yet I have to admit, with equal parts admiration and frustration, that he rose above the occasion, and not *to* it. His better self prevailed, where my lesser self was in control of my actions, and that led me to flounder.

And, to make matters worse, I allowed Zach to take the blame: blame that was mine to assume. He was being brave, and I love him for it, but I was being cowardly, and I can't help but despise myself for that.

I look for something in the Bible that will calm my nerves, assure me that what I've done isn't too terrible. But the Bible is a bit clearer on the things we shouldn't do and which should be punished, and the things we should do, which ought to be rewarded. But on the things we wish we hadn't done, I did find Philippians 3:13, which says, "One thing I do: forgetting what lies behind and straining forward to what lies ahead." First John 1:9 states, "If we confess our sins, he is faithful and just to forgive us our sins and to cleanse us from all unrighteousness."

I know I must confess my sins. *'But,'* I must ask, *'to whom? To God, who already knows them? To Deacon Kopp? He certainly will only tell me to confess them to my daed, but I know what this will mean, and I simply cannot face that.'*

'And Zach has willingly sacrificed,' I remind myself. *'Wouldn't I be disrespecting that choice, that sacrifice, by*

undoing it now, simply to appease my own conscience?'

I allow myself to be satisfied with that. But I'm still anxious to see Zach, as we haven't spoken since that horrid night in the basement. I long to feel his smile upon me, so that I know he doesn't hate me. I want to hear his voice and know that he's not embittered. I want to kiss him again.

And again.

So, the very day afterward, before Zach has even had a chance to call me and tell me what's happened at his house, I decide to stop by for a little visit. Our families don't live very far from one another, and it's not uncommon for us to pop by unannounced. That's how close we are. That's what strikes me so hard, and so low, when Ruth Yoder, Zach's mamm, greets me at the door with a sad smile, and tells me what's happened.

We linger at the door, and I find it odd, at first, that she doesn't let me in. Then, I reflect on what they must believe: that Zach had lured me into the basement to seduce me, and that I was so dangerous a temptation that Zach had to be physically removed from my presence before he disgraced the entire family.

For her to invite me in would only make them hypocrites, and, as a practical matter, won't help their relationship with Zach.

I ask where he's gone, and, of course, she doesn't tell me. She claims not to know, and I believe she might not know. But

I also know that, if she did know, she wouldn't tell me, because the last thing they want is for us to keep seeing each other.

That, sadly, seems to be the one thing everybody (but me) agrees on!

And, after all the years of fellowship, of shared Sunday services and harvest festivals, quilt auctions and Whoopie pies, Ruth Yoder smiles politely, thanks me for coming, and wishes me well. When the door closes, clicking shut, I feel a pang of loneliness like I've never known before, yet it feels oddly familiar.

'This,' I realize, *'must be what Zach felt.'*

This is what I would have felt, if the door of my own family home had ever been closed on me, that click echoing in my hollow soul.

It's a terrible feeling, but one I hope never to forget, so that I know I'll never do it to my own family. My doors will always be open.

I take a deep breath, and turn to walk back to my horse and buggy. But when I hear my name being whispered from around the side of the house, I stop and turn. Isaac approaches, looking nervously around. We share a little hug. I've known Isaac his whole life, and, in a lot of ways, I've come to feel about him as if he were my own younger brother, the one I never got to see grow up.

Isaac says, "You're looking for Zach." I nod, and he adds,

"He'll be at his friend Dylan's place. His folks are in Easton, their last name is Reed."

Isaac's name echoes in the distance, in his father's voice, and Isaac turns. "Gotta go. Tell him to contact me."

"I will." He turns, but I utter his name, and Isaac turns. Our eyes lock, and we share a single thought. We both hope he's all right. I say, "Thank you, Isaac."

He gives me a wink, then turns to join his father in the fields behind the house.

But I stop, my legs deciding I will not turn away from my responsibilities again. *Confess your sins*, the Bible said. And this may be my last chance to confess these particular sins to this particular person.

And this may be the last moment in which my confession can still make a difference, can still do some good.

I walk around the side of the Yoder house, toward the back, where John's voice came from (I'm pretty sure). Isaac sees me, and I can tell by his expression that he's nervous, as I walk toward John, hoeing the weeds in the field. Isaac's face, mouth small and low, eyebrows cramped and crooked, tells me this might not be the best idea I've ever had. But I know it's not among the worst ones either; those are why I'm doing this now.

John sees me coming, straightening up as I approach. The cold wind hits me with a little gust, as if trying to push me back. But the clouds are heavy behind me, pushing me forward.

Trapped.

As I approach, John stands waiting. He lets the silence drag on, until I have to speak. I don't have a choice, and I don't suppose I really want one.

I say, "I just heard what happened between you and Zach."

"From whom, may I ask?"

"If it's true, it hardly matters."

Now, I let a little silence pass, and John finally says, "It's true. What of it?"

I take a deep breath. "I just wanted you to know that Zach lied to my daed. It was my idea to go down into that basement. I was the one who wanted something to happen that night. Zach was totally innocent —"

"Of course you'd say that," John says.

"Really? And endanger my place in my own family? Mister Yoder, my father was ready to throw me out into the street just the day before, because he doubted my chastity. And my family ... besides Zach, my family is all I really have. And Zach knows that. He's such a kind and courageous person, I ... I can't believe I let him get into so much trouble on my account."

Now, John looks at me with some measure of belief. I can see it in his face, his eyes narrowing as he considers, jaw subtly chewing on these new and unpleasant truths. To him, they must taste of self-incrimination and shame, ashes in his mouth.

"I know Zach is uncertain of his future," I say, "but I think it should still be his decision to make, and not be forced into it by misunderstanding and presumption."

John looks me up and down, nodding slowly and muttering, "I see."

I wait for him to say more; to admit his misdeeds the way I've admitted mine, to confess his guilt, and thank me for bringing this to his attention.

But he just glares at me, until I have to clear my throat and add, "You can do whatever you wish, of course, but I hope you'll remember that I'm telling you these things in confidence; because I think it's important to your relationship with Zach that you know, that your whole family knows. But if my family finds out, I will be thrown out, and then my life will basically be over. So, however angry you are with me for trying to manipulate your son, and then lying about it; however frustrated you are that I'm the cause of something you did while misinformed, well, I hope you'll keep my confidence."

"Since your father's attack on my son's integrity," John says, "we are no longer speaking."

"And I hope you can return to speaking terms. My daed is a good man, he admires and respects you. I'm sorry that your friendship with him is still another casualty of my dishonesty. But if you do speak —"

"I'm not one to betray a confidence, Katie." I smile, but it's premature. "However, I'm not one to lie, either. If asked, I must tell the truth. If not, there is nothing compelling me to volunteer it."

I nod, as his stern reply sinks in. It's the most I'm going to get, so I take it with gratitude, and turn to cross the field before he changes his mind. I see Isaac again on the way; I give him a little nod and he returns it, each reassuring the other that everything will be all right.

Somehow.

I decide to take the buggy to the library. I'm not that great at using the internet, but it's really not too terribly hard, once you get the librarian to virtually walk you through every step. I've seen the internet before, of course (though only a fraction of it, and I'm sure not the gross parts that are the most popular), and it doesn't take me long to find the Reeds' address, and even a little map with directions.

I love how the world is changing so fast!

It takes two hours in the buggy to get to the Reed residence in Easton. It's a lovely two-story brick house, two cars in the driveway (two!) and no place to park the buggy. This narrow residential street, shimmering from the rain during this break in the showers, wasn't made for buggies like mine, or lifestyles like ours.

After creating a bit of an unintentional stir, Zach comes out and gives me a big, surprised hug and kiss, right there in front of Dylan, and God, and everyone. He introduces me to the pleasant-looking Dylan, tall and very fit, blue eyes peeking out from behind his shaggy blond hair. He's very sweet and very polite, parking their cars on the street so I can park the horse and buggy on the driveway.

It's not long before I'm an invited guest in their home.

It's so different inside the Reed home. Framed family photos hang on the walls: smiling faces looking out from roller coaster carts, river bank inner tubes, school plays. A huge television dominates one wall of the living room. Music plays on the stereo, softly, and nobody seems to be really listening to it. But it plays anyway, nonstop.

In the Englischer world, something seems to always be on, no matter what: stereo, TV, internet; it hardly seems to matter.

Zach is somber, as he tells me what happened with his daed. "I'm so sorry, Zach, it's my fault. I should have told the truth from the very first, down in that basement —"

"No, Katie, things have worked out just the way you said they would." Reading my confusion, he adds, "I'm just where God wants me to be."

"Living in a pal's basement is where God wants you to be?" I turn to Dylan. "No offense, it's really a very nice basement, but —"

"No worries," Dylan says with a smile, holding his hand

out to calm my fears. "You're right, and we won't be here long."

I turn to Zach, and wait for an explanation. He says, "The University at Columbia, Missouri."

"You ... you got accepted so quickly?"

"Not precisely," Zach says. "But it's a haven for ex-Amish: they have all kinds of support systems, financial aid; and word is I'm bound to get into classes next semester, if not this one. That'll give me time to get established in a job somewhere, a place to live ..."

I turn to Dylan, more curious than demanding, of his part in all this. "Good school for us Englishmen too."

"Englischers," Zach reminds him.

"Right. Anyway, they've got one of the best Comparative Religions programs in the country." Dylan smiles, raising his hands, palms up. "And I tell you, ask, and it will be given to you; seek, and you will find; knock, and it will be opened to you. For everyone who asks, receives, and the one who seeks finds, and to the one who knocks, it will be opened."

I say, "Luke 11:9-10."

"Very good," Dylan says, with an impressed nod.

"He's right," Zach says, "it's gonna be great ... except for one thing." After a little silence and a hopeful smile, he adds, "You."

"Zach?"

"Come with me, Katie!"

"Oh, Zach, I can't —"

"Of course you can," Zach says, looking deep into my eyes. "You know I'm right, that there's a whole big world out there for us. We don't have to choose, we can have it all."

"*You* don't have to choose," I say, "but *I* do! My family —"

"And they'll always be your family, Katie. But what about *our* family?"

"We can have that here! Zach, just because your father told you to go doesn't mean you have to! Stay, and we'll raise our family here! You and your daed'll come together in time. You said he wasn't mad, just ..."

"Like a stranger," Dylan says.

"But he's not a stranger, Zach," I say, "and if you stay, and make things right between you, he doesn't have to be. But if you leave now, well ... years go by, things don't just get better. They say time heals all wounds, but, from what I've seen, those wounds don't heal right. They scar over, they fester."

Zach and Dylan exchange a glance. Zach shrugs and shakes his head.

I can't resist saying to Dylan, "You want him to go with

you to Columbia, I suppose."

"Not if he wants to stay," Dylan answers, with no show of temper.

I look at Zach, and he back at me, the silence getting heavier. But he says nothing, and I feel the breath being sucked out of my lungs. We've each made our plea to the other, and neither seems ready to give up their ground.

Trapped.

Dylan says, "If you two don't mind my butting in, I think what you both need to do right now, is take some time to pray on this, reflect, and digest. We're not leaving for another few days; there's time enough to get a little perspective."

Dylan looks at us both with a hopeful smile, putting his right hand on mine, his left hand on Zach's. The more I come to see of this Dylan, the more I like him. I can't help but think that if more Englischers were like this, there probably wouldn't be such a big chasm between our cultures.

'Then again,' I have to tell myself, *'for all you know, they all could be like this. When did you ever give them a chance?'*

That nagging, doubting voice plagues me on the buggy ride back home, the light drizzle hinting at another torrent soon to come.

Maybe I've been turned around on this all along, I have to admit. *Maybe the world out there isn't just a horror show, a mad carnival of predators and liars, as I've been told. Maybe it's not such a scary place, the outside world. Maybe it's time I opened my mind and my heart, as much as I keep telling others to do the same.*

And I do as Dylan suggested, and as I so often suggest to others. I pray on it. I ask the Lord for strength and guidance. And then, as my daed always taught me, I take action, to allow the Lord's will to take root. To this end, of course, I go to the Bible.

But there is no easy answer, even in that great tome. The Fifth Commandment tells us, *"Honor your father and your mother, that your days may be long upon the land which the Lord your God is giving you."*

But in Genesis 1:28, God told Noah, *"'Fill the Earth and subdue it.'"*

From Matthew: *"But when they persecute you in this city, flee ye into another."* I find myself contemplating Matthew, the words of Jesus himself: *"Think not that I am come to send peace on earth: I came not to send peace, but a sword. For I am come to set a man at variance against his father, and the daughter against her mother, and the daughter-in-law against her mother-in-law. And a man's foes shall be they of his own household. He that loveth father or mother more than me is not worthy of me: and he that loveth son or daughter more than me is not worthy of me. And he that taketh not his cross, and followeth after me, is not worthy of me."*

But it only brings more questions than answers. *'Should I accept the division of my family, my separation from them, as prophesied by the Christ?'* I wonder, my mind reeling. *Or is this missive written to reassure Zach's father, and my own, that their willingness to turn away from their own children is itself a Godly turn?*

Is this the way our God wants us to treat each other? Can that be?

No! In Mark 5, Jesus said, "Go home to your family, and report to them all that the Lord has done for you, and the mercy He has shown you."

Is that to mean I should stay here and refuse Zach's invitation? My mind feels like my heart: splitting down the middle, cracking wide open, and pouring all out into the mud, wasted and tired.

Trapped.

That night at dinner, over roasted chicken and baked spaghetti squash, Esther and Martha play a little game they invented, the rules of which I can't quite make out. But they giggle and clap, twice sometimes, giggling even more.

How simple and wonderful their lives are, I can't help but reflect. *I don't think they'll ever realize how sweet and pure childhood is.*

Or how brief.

My daed clears his throat to end one conversation and begin another.

"Katie," he says, quieting the rest of the table chatter, "I've decided it's time for you to marry."

What?! I want to shout, using every bit of my strength of will not to do so. But I also don't need to.

He readily volunteers, "You're obviously of a mind to marry; you'd marry that Yoder boy in a heartbeat."

"Daniel," Mary says, "might we not discuss this in private before —?"

"Too much discussion has already come and gone," Daed says. Then, as if I'm not sitting right in front of them, he says to her, "She's obviously not prepared to make this decision on her own, and she's not prepared to govern her own actions in the meantime. I think we should take a cue from John Yoder himself, and usher things along if we can. He who hesitates is lost."

"And who am I to marry?" I ask, very soft and cold. "Am I not even allowed to know who it is, much less choose a husband for myself?"

"You will not disrespect me, Katie." After a sip of cold milk, he adds, "And you'll see that I'm right about this, as I've been right about everything else so far. And don't look at me like that, as if I'm some kind of slave trader. You will, of course, have some say in the man we choose. I was thinking about Melvin, the ironsmith's boy. He seems capable enough."

I know the boy he means, and I would never marry him, under any circumstances.

I just don't love him.

No point in trying to explain that to Daed, I realize. Love doesn't mean anything to him, at least not as he claims it does; how we all claim so much to love one another, even as we gossip and judge and manipulate. That's not love. That's not community. I'm sacrificing my life with Zach for this?

My daed goes on to say, "Or there's the Schrock boy; their farm's pigs are a stout and reliable resource —"

"Stop it," I shout, standing up from the table, "just stop it! You're not marrying me off to someone just because you're upset with me! I'm a person, a human being, and I'll make my own choices from now on!"

"Measure your words, girl!"

"I won't," I say, my voice cracking from the pressure, and the anger, "and you'll get no more of them!" I run out of the room, glad to hear my mamm trying to talk some sense into my daed in hushed tones behind me.

While my family is eating, I climb out a window, unseen, and hurry down the road a half a mile to the emergency payphone. I'm nervous as I dial the number, my fingers trembling, praying that Zach's friend will accept my collect call. The phone rings on the other end, and then clicks, as I wait for the charges to either be accepted or rejected.

Dylan picks up. "Katie? Are you okay?"

"Fine. Thank you for taking the call. Is Zach there?"

"Sure, hold on."

A brief moment and some odd noises later, Zach says, "Katie?"

"Zach." I take a deep breath, and hold it. "I've changed my mind. I want to come with you."

CHAPTER 12

I pack that night. Zach and I decide to wait until morning, and that he'll come pick me up. I'm nervous, and can hardly sleep. The thunder rumbles, the rain coming down in an even shower.

In the morning, I look up at those rolling clouds, still intense, still clinging to their dominion above us. Yet the rain falls in a teasing trickle compared to what could be, to what may be, waiting in the shadows of our immediate future, gearing up for a crushing blow.

Not yet.

I hear Mamm call my name, and I know Zach has arrived. I peek out the window and see him in his buggy, rain falling around him. My heart jumps, blood hot in my veins. My mouth goes dry, and I swallow hard before pulling myself away from the window. I remember that morning my daed was going to kick me out. He'd opened this very same door, and I'll never forget the sound of that little, fateful click, which might as well have been the crashing sound of a million boulders falling on top of me.

This time, *my hand* is the one on the door knob.

This time, the decision is mine.

I enter the living room, and see my daed and mamm standing with Zach, soaking wet, just this side of the door.

My daed says, "I forbade you to see this boy, Katie! What's the meaning of this?"

"I'm leaving with him," I say, carrying my bag across the room and toward Zach.

But Daed stops me, his fingers wrapping around my arm. "Over my dead body!"

"I won't stay here and have you treat me like some object to be traded, or sold, or given away to the next hog farmer who strolls by the farm."

"It's not like that, and you know it, Katie!"

"I don't know any such thing," I say, pulling my arm free of his grip. "But I do know I love Zach, and that I'll follow him anywhere."

"Even into the fiery pits of hell?"

A sudden churning sound gets louder fast, going from the far distance to very, very close. The house begins to creak around us, that omnipresent rumbling shaking the house, and not merely with its incredible volume. I run to the window, but I only make it a few steps before a tremendous crack fills our ears, and the house itself jostles an inch or two to the side. Unprepared, we're all nearly knocked off our feet. By the time I get to the window, the floor is already being covered by a fast-moving film of muddy water.

Outside, brown water rushes past the house, carrying chunks of fencing, and even the tops of some smaller trees.

"It's a flash flood!" I say.

'Now,' the storm says. *'You've waited long enough; and so have I.'*

Now.

Now I see the storm for what it is, not merely a collection of molecules in the air, not merely the release of water built up from the recent rains. And it's not God's wrath, as in the story of Noah. It's not even the physical manifestation of Zach's growing doubt and worry, the indefinable sadness that has plagued him.

It's me, I realize. I created this storm, or at least inspired God to use it as a way of reminding me that my sins will follow me, that my mistakes cannot merely be sloughed off or ignored. I have done wrong, and offended man and God in the doing. I didn't mean to. I'm a girl in love, and love was my only goal.

But the results are plain to see: everything is being washed away by my gathering shame. It will leave nothing behind in its terrible wake.

But beyond any metaphor, any interpretation of events from any angle, one thing is clear and undeniable: one of the two huge barn double doors has been torn away by the flash flood and rammed up against the side of the house, causing that terrific crash. It's also what made the entire structure move.

"The barn door's slammed into the house," I call out, "knocked it off the foundation, I think."

"Not off it," Daed says, "or we'd all be floating away in a pile of debris."

Not yet.

I say, "We gotta get outta here!"

The girls are screaming as Mamm and I scoop them up, holding and stroking them and trying to calm them, even as the water churns outside and the house begins to creak and buckle around us.

"The house is giving way," Zach says. "We have to evacuate!"

"Into that flood?" Daed says. "That's not just water out there, young man, but lengths of barbed wire, twisted metal, shattered wooden beams, debris of all kinds. We'll not only be drowned, but we'll be crushed, mangled!"

"What choice have we got?" Zach turns and tries to pull

the front door open, but it won't budge. "It's jammed! Must be wedged in, I'll try the back." Zach hurries across the house and to the kitchen door that leads to the backyard. Some banging and splashing tells us all in the living room two things: the back door is also jammed, and that water is filling up the kitchen as much as it is the living room, pouring in from the new cracks in the walls.

Zach returns to the living room and grabs at one of the windows, the great big scarlet oak tree not far away. He pulls the windows, but it's no use. Zach stops, looking frantically around. Daed asks him, "What's in your mind, boy?"

"Something heavy to smash the windows!"

"Use your head; we can't climb out a broken window! The glass'll cut my girls to shreds, and that current'll wash us all away!"

Zach glares at Daed, sneering unafraid. "That's as may be, Mr. Lapp, but we also don't know how long it's going to be before this whole house is torn away from its foundation and carries us all off. You think there's a lot of floating debris out there now, wait until you're stuck under two stories of it!"

Mamm cries out, "Daniel?" as the girls cry even louder. I stand in the rising tide of gushing, muddy water, slowly flooding the house. The walls wrench slightly and then stop, the awful sound of gnashing wood erupting, and then suddenly ceasing, promising a swift return.

Not yet.

"What about the basement?" Zach asks.

"The basement'll be flooding by now," I say, "and won't that door be jammed shut, too?"

"You're right, Katie." Zach looks around. "Well, we can't stay here. Let's go up to higher ground."

"And then what?" Daed asks.

Zach peers out the living room window, to the scarlet oak tree on the side of the house. "That tree should hold. Scarlet oak; looks sturdy enough."

Daed says, "You must be out of your mind."

I take a look for myself, quickly understanding how Zach's mind is working here. "Those branches are the highest ground we can reach," I say, "*if* we can reach them."

"We'd better find a way," Zach replies, "before this house gets torn away and just falls apart, drowns us all like rats." Zach looks up, the water rumbling, the house creaking, thunder rolling. "We can't get to that tree from here: too far; but if those branches hang close enough to the roof, we should be able to climb onto it from there."

"They do," mamm says, "I've been telling him to trim the tree, but he won't ... thank God!"

Zach turns to Daed. "How do we get to the roof?"

"Ladder's the only way," Daed says, "got a twenty-footer up in the attic."

"Not in the basement?"

"Too big to get up those little basement stairs. It slides out of the attic in a straight shot, right out the second story window."

"All right, then," Zach says, taking my hand. "Let's go!" Zach pulls me across the room and up the stairs. After an uncertain moment, Daed ushers Mamm and the girls up the stairs behind us. The water is rising and we all have to slog through the heavy brown filth. Daed picks up Esther, who clings to his neck, Mamm already holding the much younger Martha.

Zach and I get to the top of the stairs, just as the house shifts again, a loud and heavy "thunk" somewhere, telling us that the house's courageous battle to stand against the oncoming tide is fast being lost.

Zach and I make way for my family, and then we ladies clear the area under the attic door. Setting Esther down, Daed pulls the attic door down from the ceiling, and extends the folding ladder built onto the door. He takes the few rungs up and reaches into the dark attic, returning seconds later, and pulling one end of the twenty-foot ladder out at an angle. After about seven feet, Zach takes position under the ladder and guides the rest of it out, holding it roughly in the middle. Once the end of the ladder has cleared the attic, I fold the door ladder up and close the attic door.

To be heard above the din of the churning flood, the spray, the rain, and the wind, Daed calls to Zach, "We'll have to smash out this window, frame and all! On three!" Mamm and I step back, our hands protecting the girls' little faces, and our own. Daed counts it out, and they smash the ladder into the window. The first strike shatters the glass, sending shards whipping into the hall with the angry wind. The second blow cracks the frame on one side, and a third strike, with the end of that big ladder, sends the smashed window frame falling out of the wall entirely.

It's even louder in the hallway now, and a lot colder, with the wind blasting in through the new hole. Daed waves Zach over. Zach turns to me and crosses over and grabs the ladder, holding it horizontally over my head, so Zach can confer with Daed. The ladder's heavier than I thought it would be, and the cold wind cuts under my exposed arms.

By the new hole in the wall, Daed says to Zach, "The flood's gonna push the bottom of the ladder into the side of the house. We've gotta pitch it out far, and get the other end to jam up under the roof. It's the only way it'll hold!"

Zach turns to me as they start pushing the ladder out as far as it will go. I follow slowly, supporting the end of the ladder, as they feed the rest of it out of the whole. "We got it now, Katie," Zach calls, "let 'er go!"

I let go and step back. Zach and my daed work together,

straining to hold the ladder. Most of the ladder, and most of its weight, is sticking out of that hole, dangling over the side of the house. The two men look at each other, teeth gritted. They nod, and, at the same time, thrust the ladder out of the hole.

Zach holds onto the last rung of the ladder, and Daed holds onto Zach. The ladder's weight nearly pulls Zach out of the hole, but he holds on with a stunted grunt. As planned, the bottom of the ladder lands in the rushing water, not far from the barn door that presses against the house. The ladder sinks into the flooding waters and is pushed toward the house. From where I'm standing, I see Zach jam his end of the ladder up and under the lip of the roof, as the water pushes it forward. There's a loud wooden crack, and Zach is thrown backward, away from the hole.

"Zach!" I run to him on the floor, and help him up as he shakes his head.

"I'm fine," he says, turning to Daed. "How'd we do?"

My daed is leaning out of the hole, checking the ladder, which seems firmly in place, at just the right angle for climbing, not too sharply vertical.

Daed says, "You first."

Zach shakes his head. "We need the strongest among us to pull everyone up. You go; I'll feed 'em up the ladder and take up the rear."

They share a moment of silent deliberation, as if daed is

trying to out-think Zach, but can't. As the house creaks again, moving just a little bit further, he snaps into action. "Okay, let's go," Daed says, "up the ladder. I'll go and then help you up. Mary, you come up next; then we'll bring up the girls, then Katie and Zach." He turns to Zach. "If that's okay with you?"

Zach shrugs. "It's your house."

"It *was*."

Daed climbs out of the roof and onto the ladder. He looks down, then up, then back at Zach. "Good luck up there," Zach says.

"Don't dawdle," my daed says, before climbing the ladder. Even with the creaking of the house and the churning of the floodwaters, I can hear my daed's footsteps on the roof.

He made it!

By now, we're all gathered by the hole. I say to Mamm, "You're next; I'll hand Esther up."

Mamm nods, then pulls me in for a long, deep hug. Finally releasing me, Mamm turns and climbs unsteadily out of the hole. She grabs it, insecure, and manages to push her way on to the ladder and then climb it. I know Daed is up there to help her finish her climb.

Esther is crying as I pick her up. "No, no, please no," she says, "I'm scared, scared, scared, scared —"

I kneel to her, just five years old, and look her dead in the eye, Zach cradling the tearful Martha nearby. "Esther, listen to me. God is looking out for us, right? Right?"

"Then why is God trying to kill us?"

"God is trying to *save* us, Esther, to save us! But he needs us to do our part. Now, I know this is scary, but it's just like the monkey bars at the park. You remember the monkey bars, and you're so great at them!"

"It's too high; I'm afraid!"

The house creaks again; and whatever fear Esther has, mine is greater by a thousand. I look deep into my sister's eyes. "Listen to me, Esther: you have to do this, okay? You have to do it. Now show me how good you are on those monkey bars, right? I'll be right here, and as soon as I let go, Daed's gonna be there to scoop you up."

"You promise?"

The words catch in my throat, but I push them out. "I promise. Okay?"

Esther finally nods, and I step out with her, the winds pushing hard against us as I set her feet on one rung and her hands on the sides. "Now climb up, Esther, climb!" I have to shout, but she hears me.

And she climbs, her little legs passing awkwardly, fearfully, by each other as they push her up the ladder. I see Daed's hand reach up and grab her, yanking her up and off the ladder in a flash.

Zach hands Martha to me. He leads me to the hole. "You hold her, I'll hold you!"

I nod. My legs are quivering, nearing numbness from the sheer terror. But I know I have to take my own advice, at long last. I put my foot on the rung of the ladder and grab the side with one hand, holding Martha with the other. Daed is reaching down with his mighty hand. I climb a single rung to meet him, and he grabs Martha by the arm and pulls her up. She cries, in pain and in terror, but at least he's got her. At least she's safe.

I climb up the ladder, too; quickly, now that I'm unencumbered. The ladder slips a bit as I climb, but it holds its position against the lip of the roof that extends over the side of the house.

I get to the roof, slanted, my family clutching the wet shingles, soaked to the skin.

But alive.

I turn to see Zach climbing the ladder, but it slips again as he does, more than it did when I climbed up. *I weakened it,* I realize. *Now it's gonna give way!*

I shout, "Zach!"

Daed hears me, and crosses the roof to lean over by my side. He reaches down, fingers grasping. Zach takes another step and reaches up for Daed's hand. The men's fists grasp and lock on, just as the ladder finally does slip out from under the roof, and from under Zach. The water pushes the base of the ladder flush against the wall of the house, and the top of the ladder falls back, into the churning torrent of muddy water and floating chunks of debris.

Zach kicks against the side of the house, unable to get a foothold. The rain makes their fists slippery and I know Zach will soon fall to his death. I reach out and grab his shirt, cotton folds rising between my clawed fingers. With a great mutual heave of effort, we manage to help Zach scramble up the side of the house. Once safely on the roof, he falls in to my arms and holds me incredibly tightly, as if for dear life.

"No time for that," Daed says. "If we're gonna get to that tree, we better do it now!"

We scoot carefully along the slanted roof, to the branches of the scarlet oak next to the house. The branches closest to us are too flimsy to hold anybody's weight, and we have to break some away in order access the thicker branches further down.

Beneath us, the house shifts again. The winds seem to have died down a bit, and even the rain is letting up. But that water keeps pounding.

As before, Daed climbs onto the tree first to secure a foothold, and then bring the others aboard and off the roof. Mamm's foot slips on the wet roof as she climbs on, and Daed's strong hands pull her closer to him. He positions her on a thick branch behind him, and to the side a bit. It's a good position for her to receive her youngest daughter. And the first, Esther, is quick to jump into her daed's arms and get off that slick, crumbling roof.

The house lurches again, more than it has done before, and I know that it's only moments away from collapsing altogether. The house moans in its death throes, groaning and creaking, and gasping out its final moments upon the Earth, in what sounds like despair.

I turn to climb onto the branch, but something makes me turn again, holding onto Zach, not wanting to leave him behind again, remembering what happened the last time.

"Hurry," he says, "I'll be right behind you!"

So I turn and step carefully from the roof onto the branches. Daed grabs my hand and pulls me toward him. It's a swift move, and it nearly throws me off balance, but his superior strength and determination give him the advantage, and he manages to position me safely in the branches with Mamm and the girls.

We all turn, as the house finally gives, a hideous sound of crunching, splintering wood, copper pipes bending and twisting and pulling and popping. There are too many sounds to know them all, and all have become too much to ignore.

But it's not the sound that worries me now, sending a shock of terror through my body that numbs my brain and deadens my limbs. I can only reach out in absolute helplessness.

The house is pushed away from its foundation and begins to stream away from us, carried by the powerful current. But, without its foundation, the house crumbles fast, just as Zach knew it would. It's barely a few feet away before the roof buckles, falling into the crumbling house beneath it.

Zach jumps, hands grabbing a low-lying branch of the oak, just as the house falls away from beneath him. He swings on that soaking branch, wood cracking, one hand slipping, legs kicking. Beneath him, the churning waters of death race by, eager to consume him.

If he falls, I know I'll never see him again.

I lurch out to help him, but Daed holds out his hand to stop me. "No!" he barks, sneering with grim determination. "I'll go."

But even daed is stopped where he is, to see Zach pull his legs up and wrap them around the branch, ankles interlocking. Hanging upside-down, he begins to inch his way along the branch. His hands slip, but his legs hold. He dangles for a moment, locked ankles his only hold on this life, and that is slipping away by the second.

I watch, helpless. '*Well*,' I have to remind myself. *'Not completely helpless.'*

I start praying.

Please, Lord, send your angels to help Zach. Don't turn your back on us now. I may not know or understand your ways, but you know and understand mine. I'm a good person, Lord; Zach is a good person. Between the two of us, I'm the one who deserves to be punished, not Zach. Please don't let him pay for my mistakes, not again, not like this. This price is too high, but if either of us should pay it, let that person be me.

Zach regains his hold on the branch, and keeps working his way down toward us. Zach struggles to right himself, finally pulling himself onto the top of the branch, instead of merely dangling from it. He looks at me, at us, and nods with a smile, to show us that he's secure. We all look back from our ad hoc nest in the scarlet oak, which once stood by our house, and now doesn't stand near anything at all.

But it shelters us, and protects us, a great hand rising up out of the churning chaos of disaster, like the Hand of God itself.

The words of 1 Peter 5:6 echo in my memory: *"Humble yourselves, therefore, under the mighty hand of God so that at the proper time he may exalt you."*

We're saved, rescued; no longer trapped.

Free.

And in that tree, so wet and exposed, without even the coverage of leaves to comfort us, I feel like the time has come to open up completely. I clear my throat, gather up my courage, and say, "Daed?" Once I have his attention, I decide it's too late to go back. "Daed, I have to tell you that ... I lied to you, in the basement, when Zach was sleeping over."

Daed considers it, saying, "I don't understand; you barely said anything the entire time. It was Zach who —"

"Zach confessed to protect me," I say, "but it was my idea to sneak down to that basement."

"But he approved; helped you decide upon the details of your clandestine meeting —"

"No, Daed," I say, "Zach didn't know a thing about it. He woke up to see me standing there, and he was as surprised as you were." Daed sits in his shame, his conscience caught between his self-righteousness and his self-loathing. I go on to say, "And he wasn't going to take me, he wouldn't have allowed me in his cot that night, because he has too much respect for me, for my family, and our place in the community. He knows how much that means to you, to everyone around here ... but him."

Daed thinks about it, chewing on his regret. He looks at Zach, a branch away. "My apologies, son." I'm not surprised to hear him use that word; these two men have just faced death together, worked shoulder-to-shoulder, to save his wife and kids. Whatever Zach may have done, or may not have done. He risked his life to save us, and my daed isn't about to forget it.

Neither will I, even if a memory is all I'm left with.

Clutching the branch tighter now, as if for strength, or

merely a sense of desperate security, I say, "You hate me now."

My daed looks at me, a new expression his face: shock, horror, a sad frown, topped with yellow eyes, verging on tears.

"No, Katie, of course not. Never. Even ... even if it ever seemed that way, it was only love, and concern. I'll never apologize for loving you, or worrying for your soul and your happiness." The rains begin to let up, the sky lightening in the east. "But for letting you feel that way, I do apologize, Katie."

We cling to those branches, as much as we cling to each other. Mamm's voice is the first to puncture the eerie, growing stillness of our release. "If I speak in the tongues of men and of angels, but have not love, I am a noisy gong or a clanging cymbal." I know the scripture immediately, 1 Corinthians: 1-13, among my family's favorite passages. She speaks it with such truth in her voice, the wisdom of such terrible and recent experience, that she moves me to tears. But these are tears of love, tears of joy. "And if I have prophetic powers, and understand all mysteries and all knowledge, and if I have all faith, so as to remove mountains, but have not love, I am nothing. If I give away all I have, and if I deliver up my body to be burned, but have not love, I gain nothing."

My daed continues the scripture, his eyes on me, on us all: "Love is patient and kind; love does not envy or boast; it is not arrogant or rude. It does not insist on its own way; it is not irritable or resentful; it does not rejoice at wrongdoing, but rejoices with the truth. Love bears all things, believes all things, hopes all things, endures all things."

In a voice, both powerful and exhausted, Zach says, "Love never ends. As for prophecies, they will pass away; as for tongues, they will cease; as for knowledge, it will pass away. For we know in part and we prophesy in part, but when the perfect comes, the partial will pass away. When I was a child, I spoke like a child, I thought like a child, I reasoned like a child. When I became a man, I gave up childish ways. For now we see in a mirror dimly, but then face to face. Now I know in part; then I shall know fully, even as I have been fully known."

And it is for me to finish the scripture, the words so natural and flowing on my tongue, it is as if I have been waiting my whole life to say them, as if I am saying them for the first time: "So now faith, hope, and love abide, these three; but the greatest of these is love."

Together, we rise up in a unified, "Amen," and retire into the quiet reflection of the storm's passing. The flood waters slow down beneath us, the winds relaxing. I cling to that tree, knowing that the worst has passed. But what lays ahead, I still do not know.

CHAPTER 13

After several hours, Deacon Kopp pulls up in a motor boat with several uniformed officers, who turn out to be firefighters. There's enough room for us all, and we finally climb down out of that life-saving scarlet oak. We spend the night in a nearby shelter, eating canned chicken noodle soup, stale saltine crackers, and hardening mild cheddar cheese.

It's one of the best meals I've ever had.

The next day, the citizens of Faith's Landing get together, to discuss plans to clean and rebuild. Auctions will be held to raise money; crafts and foods will have to be created.

But first, we hold a massive prayer service to celebrate our survival of this terrible test, to thank God for seeing us through it, and to thank each other for being here to receive us on the other end, the light at the end of Faith's Landing's muddy tunnel.

It's at this meeting that Zach takes me aside. Our departure for Columbia, Missouri, was postponed, of course, and may still be held off for a day or two, but no more than that, or Zach and Dylan will definitely lose their chance at classes this semester. The time to leave begins to loom once more.

But not for me. I can't leave my family behind now, when we've lost our home. As joyful as I am at our survival, I am also saddened at the loss around me: our family home, and the homes of the others who were caught in the path of this disaster. It would be selfish and wrong to leave, and I have been that entirely too much lately. I'm correcting it step by step, however. As the old spiritual goes, "I'm not what I ought to be, but I'm better than I used to be."

I'm only saddened that I won't be able to be that for Zach. I have to sacrifice him and his love, his company, and the family we might have had together. But my heart leaves no room for doubt on this matter, not anymore.

I'm also glad that Zach and his daed have repaired their relationship, just as me and my daed have ours. Even our two fathers patched things up, brought together by the truth, and by the grace of God. I reflect on how trials like these manage to bring us together, make us stronger; that is, if they fail to destroy us completely.

But a sad fact seems indisputable and insurmountable. We've done our very best, but our destinies are calling us in different directions now, to lonely roads leading further and further apart, until there is a last look, a parting glance, and no more for ever after.

At least Zach has straightened things out with his own father, and in fact both my daed and Zach's have repaired their friendship. So, it seems I will carry most of the burden of Zach's departure, which only seems just, in a tragically poetic sort of way.

So when Zach steps over to me, I feel that familiar cold stone sinking in my gut, that awful feeling that everything I'd ever dreaded is about to happen, and that there is absolutely nothing I can do about it.

I start, unable to wait and hear him drag it out, making my unendurable pain almost eternal. "Zach, I —"

"No, Katie, listen to me for a minute." He puts one hand each of my arms, palms gently pressing. "I can't tell you how happy I was when you said you wanted to come with me. I felt as if every dream I'd ever had was coming true, all at once. I haven't had many dreams come true, Katie, and I have to say it felt to me like God's will at work, finally rewarding my time of trial, giving me the promotion I'd worked so hard for."

I say nothing. I know where he's going with this; he's making sure I'll still go.

But I won't.

He says, "I think about living without you, about leaving you behind, and it makes me physically ill, Katie; like I can feel my heart breaking, straight down the middle. I thank God every minute that I've been spared that fate, thank God that you've agreed to stay by my side, no matter what."

'Please don't,' I silently plead. *'For the love of God, you're making this too painful. How can I look into your eyes now, and tell you the things I know I have to say? Why do you have to make it so painful? Why did I have to be so clumsy with our love and our lives? Why do I have to love you so much?'*

Zach says, "But the thing is, I don't think we should go."

Wait, what?

I can't hold it back: "Wait, what?"

"Look around you, Katie. The community needs us, your family needs us. We certainly can't go anywhere until they're back on their feet."

"Oh, Zach, I —"

"And there's a lot of cleanup. I just wouldn't feel right, leaving like this. And, coming so close to seeing it all get washed away, I dunno, it did something to me. They say you never appreciate what you've got until it's gone. Well, Faith's Landing isn't gone, Katie. It's still here, and so should we be."

Oh, Zach, you wonderful man! Of course we can stay, this is what I want! Oh, thank you, Lord, for showing Zach the light. Thank you Isaac, Dylan and everyone!

But I can't. I can barely breathe, much less speak a word, and much less say all of that. So I kiss him, full on the lips, our noses pressing against one another, his eyelashes tickling my brows, his nose rubbing against mine.

It's a perfect kiss, and a kiss that promises so many more to come.

I say, "What about your education, your experiences?"

Zach smiles. "I've learned plenty, and experienced even more. Anyway, there's always the library, right? Or are you going to renege on our weekly date?"

"Well, unless something better comes up ..."

"Maybe this will help clear your schedule." He pulls something small out of his pocket and hands it to me: a small, white card.

I take a closer look; it's a library card. "Oh, Zach, that's so sweet ..." Then I read the name on the card.

Mrs. Katie Yoder.

By the time I look back at Zach, he's gazing into my eyes with a sweet and knowing smile. In a very warm and loving voice, he says, "Katie Lapp, would you marry me?"

I stand before him, and I almost feel like my legs are going to give out. My heart skips, my skin tingling. My brain starts to buzz, blood rushing excitedly through my veins.

"Yes, Zachariah," I say, trying to contain my soul-bursting excitement and maintain the dignity and decorum that the moment demands. So, in that spirit, I offer him a nod and go on to say, "Yes, I will marry you."

He smiles, wrapping his arms around me, and pulling me in for a long and loving kiss. We're attracting glances from the others, but neither of us cares. When one mumbles to the other what he overheard, and as that word of our upcoming marriage spreads, our friends and neighbors actually give us a round of applause, crackling around us in a happy celebration of our love. But to me, there is only the two of us, me and Zach, together for now, and for all times, as it was meant to be. This is our moment, these are our lives. This is our home.

And it always will be.

THE END.

THANK YOU FOR READING!

And thank you for supporting me as an independent author. I hope you enjoyed reading this as much as I loved writing it! If so, you can read a sample of the next book in the next chapter.

Lastly, if you enjoyed this book and want to continue to support my writing, please leave me a review to let everyone know what you thought of my work. It's the best thing you can do to keep indie authors like me writing. (And if you find something in the book that – YIKES – makes you think it deserves less than 5-stars, drop me a line at gr8godis76@gmail.com and I'll fix it if I can.)

All the best,

RUTH PRICE

THE SHADOW OF DEATH

When a tragic loss strikes at the heart of seventeen-year-old Katie Lapp's home, will she find the strength to save her family? Or will depression, rage and loss of faith lead Katie's mamm to make a final, horrifying mistake?

After seventeen-year-old Katie Lapp's family home is swept away in a flash flood, she believes the worst is over. Katie and Zach, the man she loves, are planning their marriage, and while it's been difficult for her daed, Daniel, to believe in Zach's commitment to stay and build a life with Katie in their Amish community of Faith's Landing, slowly, the two stubborn men are coming to an understanding. But when a tragic loss strikes at the heart of Katie's home, will Katie, with Zach's help, find the strength to hold her family together? Or will depression, rage and loss of faith lead Katie's mamm to make a final, horrifying mistake?

CHAPTER ONE

Mud still cakes the streets of Faith's Landing. We've been cleaning and rebuilding for weeks, but traces of the flash flood are still everywhere. Piles of smashed pine planks, heavy with fungus, clutter the gutters. The shops along Freemans Avenue, where the land dips a bit, are still empty, and some haven't even managed to replace their shattered windows.

"Such a shame," my mamm says, as we sit around a fresh, unfinished quilt in our own new living room. Our house had been completely washed away in the flood, one of the few houses to be so afflicted, and our neighbors gathered to help us rebuild. After only a few weeks, the house is taking shape; frame and walls, windows and plumbing, floors and roof. The basics are all here.

But it's not the same, of course. What makes a house a home is the people, and we are all grateful that the people were spared, even if the house had to be sacrificed. But there was so much else; our furniture, clothes, plates, and sundries and necessities, even keepsakes and books (though we never did keep many of them) are not only gone forever, but some of those things just cannot be replaced.

I never knew how much that old house meant to me, until we lost it, and now I feel as if an old friend has died. And I know life goes on for the living, and one should never obsess over death too much. But it still feels vaguely sad and strange to be living in this new, and disconcertingly empty, house.

My youngest sister, Martha, two-years-old, is napping.

And Esther, who turned six just after the flash flood, started her first year of school the beginning of the month, so Mamm and I make the most of these quiet hours to get as much quilting done as we can. It's one of our stronger sources of revenue, and though we don't pursue wealth with any kind of vigor, we still have to do our part to raise the funds needed to heal Faith's Landing and her citizens, get us all back on our feet.

"Mamm?" She looks up, and I ask, "What's a shame?"

"The flood, of course. That old house; your daed built me that house, built *us* that house."

"And now he's built us *this* one," I say, trying to keep a cheerful tone, "along with Zach and the others."

Mamm smiles and gazes off. "Yes, Zach. He's quite a young man, isn't he?" She looks over, and we share a smile, the only answer I need to give her. Mamm looks down at her hands, as progress on the quilt marches forward. "You'll be taking your kneeling vow in October, and, once the harvest is over, come November, we'll have the wedding right here. That should refresh the family air in this place." Sadness seems to overtake her, a smile running away from her face. "'Course, then you'll be moving into a house of your own." Though we all know it's the way of things, for *kinner* to grow up and step out into the world, since my brother's death, my mamm has kept us closer to her apron strings than most.

"You still have the girls," I hurry to reassure her. "They'll need your love and attention for many long years to come. And,

Mamm, so will I; getting Zach and my new home together, not to mention when I have kinner of my own."

Her smile returns, but it seems weak, tenuous. "Now that you've decided to stay here in Faith's Landing, it doesn't really matter to me which house you live in. I'm so relieved Zach decided to stay."

'You're not the only one,' I want to say, but don't. My mamm is always to be treated with respect; that's how we were raised and that's how things should be, but my mamm has never been a terribly strong person. Since my brother's death, she relies on my daed's strength, and on mine; and on our care, too. As much as she looks after my sisters, and the house, it's always seemed to me that she needed someone to look after her; and she always had that. In Daed.

In me.

And with Faith's Landing holding us all together, my Mamm will have what she needs, at least as long as I have anything to say about it...

***

My daed, Daniel Lapp, is with Zach, his brother Isaac, and their daed John, rebuilding the Public Library. The building hasn't been destroyed, and a lot of the books have been saved, but the flooring needs to be replaced. The three men stand in a rough line, pulling up the rotting floorboards, to put them in a pile outside.

"Must be difficult for you," Daniel says to Zach.

"Mr. Lapp?"

"To see the library torn up like this, so many books lost. I know that all means a lot to you; books and learning and the like."

Zach takes in my daed's disapproving tone, but shrugs it off. They've been through a lot, and Zach hopes he's earned the older man's respect. Daniel Lapp just isn't a very easy person to know, and Zach has had to make allowances in order to get along with his soon to be father-in-law.

And one of those allowances is that Daniel Lapp has his opinions; and while he's not closed to changing them, it's an uphill battle, at the very least. If it hadn't been for the flash flood, and Zach and Daniel working together to save his wife, me, and two younger sisters in the Spring, Zach doubts they'd have even managed to forge this current, albeit uneasy, alliance.

True, Zach has shown himself to be committed and loyal, not only to me and my family, but to the entire town. But before that, he'd been vocal in his doubts, and while most people would understand and forgive, and maybe even sympathize with those doubts, my daed has never been one of those types of people.

Zach recognizes this, but he's strong in his own convictions. He expects he'll wear Daniel down eventually, so it's easy enough for Zach to look around the dimly lit library, so empty and almost ghostlike, and simply shrug off its loss. "It'll be back soon enough, Daniel. And books, learning, education, thought, philosophy, history, science, religion…these things aren't going anywhere."

"Well you're right about that, at least as far as religion goes. Those other things are fine for some people, I suppose."

"But not for you?"

Daniel looks Zach over, up and down, while Isaac, Zach's brother, listens from nearby. Isaac isn't usually one to eavesdrop, but he's too courteous to enter a private conversation, and too observant simply not to notice. Daniel says to Zach, "There are only a few things in this life that mean anything to me, Zachariah. My daughter is first among them."

The air is heavy with mold, the musty stench clinging to the dust that cakes Zach's nose and throat. The floorboards are laden with moisture and mold, and they crackle with clouds of dust and spores, as the men pull them up from the foundation.

Daed says, "We'll see, come November."

"You'll see us married, come November."

"I should hope so, young man. Let's hope your tendency toward second thoughts doesn't put you on another road, abandoning us and leaving my daughter heartbroken…

End of The Shadow of Death – Preview!

THANK YOU FOR READING!

And thank you for supporting me as an independent author. I hope you enjoyed reading this as much as I loved writing it!

If so, look for this book in eBook or Paperback format at your favorite online book distributors. Also, when a series is complete, we usually put out a discounted collection. The best deal for this series is to purchase Amish Faith Through Fire, which includes the first three collections and a bonus short story by Ruth Price. If you'd rather read the entire series at once and save a few bucks doing it, we recommend looking for the Amish Faith Through Fire collection.

Lastly, if you enjoyed this book and want to continue to support my writing, please leave me a review to let everyone know what you thought of my work. It's the best thing you can do to keep indie authors like me writing. (And if you find something in the book that – YIKES – makes you think it deserves less than 5-stars, drop me a line at gr8godis76@gmail.com and I'll fix it if I can.)

All the best,

RUTH PRICE

ABOUT THE AUTHOR

Ruth Price is a Pennsylvania native and devoted mother of four. After her youngest set off for college, she decided it was time to pursue her childhood dream to become a fiction writer. Drawing inspiration from her faith, her husband and love of her life Harold, and deep interest in Amish culture that stemmed from a childhood summer spent with her family on a Lancaster farm, Ruth began to pen the stories that had always jabbered away in her mind. Ruth believes that art at its best channels a higher good, and while she doesn't always reach that ideal, she hopes that her readers are entertained and inspired by her stories.

Manufactured by Amazon.ca
Bolton, ON